CW01214424

ELLIOT J HARPER

The Strange Tales of Gillion

Copyright © 2024 by Elliot J Harper

All rights reserved. No part of this publication may be reproduced, stored or transmitted in any form or by any means, electronic, mechanical, photocopying, recording, scanning, or otherwise without written permission from the publisher. It is illegal to copy this book, post it to a website, or distribute it by any other means without permission.

This novel is entirely a work of fiction. The names, characters and incidents portrayed in it are the work of the author's imagination. Any resemblance to actual persons, living or dead, events or localities is entirely coincidental.

Elliot J Harper asserts the moral right to be identified as the author of this work.

Visit www.elliotjharper.com for more information.

Book cover provided by Castle and Classics.

First edition

ISBN: 9798333195722

This book was professionally typeset on Reedsy.
Find out more at reedsy.com

For Dad

"We live on a placid island of ignorance in the midst of black seas of infinity, and it was not meant that we should voyage far."

H.P. Lovecraft

Contents

Acknowledgments

I would like to thank Ross Jeffrey, Nigel Walker, Robert Welbourn, Ian Craven, Nicola Keat, Anthony Self, Andrew Stevenson, Julie Farrah, David Young, and Stephanie Harper for their help at the beta reading stage. Without their insight, this collection might not have been.

1

The Summoning

The tranquil and somewhat somnolent village of Gilramore was but a half day's journey from the thick smog of Arcton in the horseless carriage, or, if money was no object, a mere hour-long jaunt in the dirigible. It was the last marker before entering the dense woodlands that dominated the region, and of which housed a secret place known only to the few, to the wealthy, and to the initiated.

A dirigible puttered past the village, entirely unobserved by its sleeping inhabitants. It soared over a vast carpet of dark spruce, before tracking a private road. It was occupied by Jessalyn Fitzsimons. She was of noted stock, evidenced by her extravagant mode of transport. Her family had become wealthy upon the back of the business of textiles, chiefly procuring the materials from the protectorate islands of Westria at a pittance, before selling the goods to the fashion houses of the capital. Their most notable buyer was Proctor and Hobbs, who ordered all their fabric from the company. Jessalyn had an adequate head for business, a necessity in Gillion when you had inherited a great fortune, but she was far better at delegation, leaving the quotidian tasks of the company to her many loyal employees. The arrangement allowed her to partake in more, shall we say, nefarious pastimes.

"Wait here until I have concluded my business," said Jessalyn crisply to her driver, Mr Aubert.

She had instructed him never to pry in her affairs, so rather than asking questions, he pulled out his newspaper, The Arcton Gazette, and proceeded to read about matters of the capital, the scandals, and the gossip that seemed to be the vogue of the times, and left her to her privacy.

Jessalyn made her way across the lawn, dashing over the moist grass, arrayed in the foggy swirl and whirl of late summer in the month of Qodes. The fissured moon peeked through the thick clouds, the jagged slit a dark crack upon its sparkling white surface, briefly illuminating her passage. Although the evening hadn't called for it, she wore her most stylish attire, a woman's business suit comprising of a blue and green tweed dress and jacket. Upon her head, she had fixed a bonnet which held her curled, flaxen hair in place, crafted from a similar material as her suit, and, of course, all acquired from Proctor and Hobbs. She gripped her bonnet as she traversed the sodden ground. She moved swiftly for her slight frame and departed the soggy sward, startling a rabbit from its nightly jaunt and sending it scurrying into the black.

As Jessalyn walked over finely wrought stonework, she glanced up at the perfidious structure that marked the end of her journey. Although beautiful in the sunlight, she always found the building rather sinister at nightfall. Watton Manor was a great many floors tall, unashamedly wide, and inhabited a vast ground, nestled within the dense woodland. A single road was the only conduit to that very spot, culminating with a heavy iron gate, which could only be admitted by invitation.

Watton Manor wasn't on any maps of Gillion. There were no discussions in the local newspapers of what might be within those dark stone walls. Of course, there was a smidgen of gossip and rumour in Gilramore about what might lie beyond the iron-wrought gates that sat at the end of the mysterious road. But no one dared speak any further on the matter, lest they receive a nightly visit from a stern-faced solicitor, who would advise them, in no uncertain terms, to keep their mouths sealed and their opinions to themselves. The Manor was a secret, clandestinely left out of the myriad speculation of the broadsheets in Arcton, and only known to the inducted.

Jessalyn was one of the few. Her father was a member of the Order, and so was her grandmother before him. Every affiliate of the nebulous fraternity was inducted via their blood and the good graces of the Watton family, which in that incarnation was presided over by one Xavier Watton and had been for many decades. Xavier was the elder statesman of the Order and ruled with an iron fist. Should anyone have dared to breathe a word of their meetings, they would have been summarily destroyed, for he had the means to do so, no matter who was on the receiving end of the ex-communication. The Watton's were an old family, wealthy before wealth was fashionable. Their business, which spanned many different industries and continents, was centred around that of the Fair Isle and its progress. It was whispered that the advancement of the nation was only secondary to their true purpose, of which was to come to fruition on that very evening.

All of that flitted around Jessalyn's fraught mind as she approached the Manor. Usually, she was robust in her demeanour, having dealt with a great many challenges in her life, but nerves fluttered in her stomach. It was the night of the Summer Solstice in a most profitable year for Gillion, and an exceedingly important moment for the Order of Malfaek. Tonight, they would perform the Summoning.

Her nomadic thoughts were disturbed when she came to the towering black doors of the Manor, where she was noted by the doorman inside. He opened the heavy frame so she could dash inside and out of the musty night.

"Am I the last?" asked Jessalyn of the man, a rotund fellow who she could never recall the name of.

"You are, Miss Fitzsimon," he replied. "The Lady Nevil arrived but a moment ago and has only just made her way downstairs. You are the last by a fraction, but I doubt it will be noted."

"Thank you," said Jessalyn as he handed her the black velvet robes. "Is everything arranged?"

"Yes, Miss Fitzsimon, all is in order," said the doorman, gesturing towards the staircase.

The doorman led Jessalyn towards the spacious marble staircase, but veered to the right, where he then guided her through an inconspicuous door into a small, empty room. There, he gripped an unlit sconce on the unadorned wall and pulled. The clangour of hidden clockwork filled her ears, followed by the rattling of chains, until a concealed door opened. It revealed a narrow staircase that spiralled downward. The doorman inclined his head towards her and motioned with his outstretched palm. She curtly took the cue, having never been fond of mummery, but she knew it was necessary in the circumstances, no matter how foolish. She handed her bonnet to the doorman, slipped the dark cloak over her clothing, and then plunged down the steps. The curved walls were littered with flickering sconces, which filled her vicinity with a cloying scent that clung to her clothes. She paid it no mind as she descended into the depths beneath the Manor.

At the nadir, Jessalyn emerged into a roughly hewn tunnel lit by more sconces. There, she lifted the cloak's hood over her head, obscuring her winsome features. Now that she was correctly attired for the Summoning, she strode through the cavern, a subterranean network of caves and tunnels that crisscrossed the depths below Watton Manor. Even then, after many previous visits for meetings and supplications, she still hesitated her forward trajectory to marvel at the vastness of the space. It was strewn with conjoining stalagmites and stalactites that dripped their reality into being, glittering as they stood guard over that furtive place. She allowed herself a brief moment to wonder at the awesome power of nature, and then continued onward, her footfalls echoing in her ears.

As Jessalyn negotiated the uneven path, she saw she was the last to arrive. The rest of the Order waited, all nine of them, her being the tenth, standing in a circle around the central firepit that gyrated with flames. All wore the unassuming black cloaks of their position, except Xavier, whose cloak was trimmed with a hint of crimson, heralding his position as leader of their surreptitious society. Here was some of the most powerful patricians in all of Gillion. If something was to have befallen in that cavern, say some disaster or attack, the banks and businesses of the nation would have gone begging for months, possibly years, until the various estates were organised, and the vast inheritances dealt with. All except her own fortune, which would be a far more challenging endeavour.

The Fitzsimons were an industrious sort, but not particularly fertile, for Jessalyn was the last of her affluent line. Her mother, Petunia, went to her grave with grief at the fact of her daughter's stoic refusal to marry one of the buffoons that were paraded before her. She had no interest in marriage or the trappings it entailed, much to the lamentation of her mother, but she believed she had found a way to circumnavigate that rather prickly issue.

She cast all thoughts aside as she came to the circle, closing it with her presence. The firepit was but the centre. The rest of the circle, of which they encapsulated, was bedecked with the Holy Script, in concentric rings, growing in intensity as it wound ever outward until the words met the feet of the Order. She only had the faintest of grasps of what it might say. None of it was written in Gillion, or any of the myriad languages of the continent of Ecrium for that matter. It was an ancient tongue. Some said it was older than the universe itself, in the time of fire and chaos. It was rumoured that it was understood by a disreputable few in the wen of Memrass Nera. Jessalyn didn't know the truth of that, having never been to that most decadent of conurbations in the sweltering southern hemisphere. She told herself she would one day visit the original home of the cult that had spawned her Order, but she knew she would never truly take the long and arduous trip. She had heard too many extraordinary stories of the metropolis and feared what she might see there, so far away from the comforts of Gillion.

Jessalyn joined the others in bowing her head and clasped her hands together so the folds of the arms of her cloak seamlessly joined. A moment passed while she pondered on what was about to occur, her pulse quickening. The tension rose, and it was as if the very air itself prickled with anticipation.

At the appointed time, Xavier unclasped his hands and lifted them to the cavern ceiling, raising his obscured head upwards, and recited the opening words of supplication. His voice was plangent and carried throughout the cavern, the faint echo reverberating off the stalagmites and stalactites, a rippling of sound as if the very gods themselves whispered back.

"Oh, Malfaek the Merciful," boomed Xavier, "we honour you today with our presence and with an offering. For many years we have waited for this moment. You, the Lord of Void, the King of Beyond, the Receiver of Souls, and our most revered of deities. We beseech you to listen to our praise, hear our reverence, and come forth and show your true self to your most humble servants." He halted and gestured towards the dark to his right. "Please, oh, Malfaek the All-Seeing, except this modest donation as proof of our devotion to you, the Great and the Wise, the first and foremost of Old Divinities. Please, hear our praise."

From the darkness, two of Watton's minions, cloaked in a lesser, darkened fabric, dragged a man. He was naked except for a loincloth of white material and senseless as he was hauled by his arms towards the circle. Jessalyn didn't know the fellow, but she had been through the process so many times in the past that it held no shock to her any longer. It was clear in the scant scriptures the Order of Malfaek had obtained that their god would receive only physical and living offers of human beings. For Malfaek was the deity of death, and he who received the souls of those most recently departed into his warm bosom. Only flesh sated him. The Order had made those offerings for decades, always on that same day, the Summer Solstice, and always in the form of an unwilling man or woman.

The foundation of the information had been sourced from a renowned hierophant at the turn of the last century by Xavier's grandfather at great expense. The fellow had apparently told that Malfaek would only come forth if one hundred offerings were made on the eve of the Solstice every year. The fellow gave the information grudgingly and under pain of death, but scriptures found later, and at even more expense, seemed to concur with his assessment.

And so, it had fallen upon Xavier and the Order, comprised from the most notable of citizens of the time. The honour was given to Jessalyn, and she would not forget it, even if the business was grisly, but in her mind, the offerings were a paltry thing compared to what might be given in return. For Malfaek the Eternal, esteemed even amongst the Old Divinities, had power over life and death. It was said he could grant those who were worthy absolution from that most infinite of slumbers. That was why she was there, the same as the rest. Her mother was mistaken, she thought, a smug grin playing on her lips, she would not need an heir.

Jessalyn's heart quickened, and she could barely contain her glee, even as the offering awakened and began to pathetically sob and shriek for succour. But his protestations were for naught. No one would come to his aid. The man was dragged across the uneven, damp floor and held fast in front of the dancing flames of the fire pit.

With the man now in place, Xavier returned his hands to the heavens and began anew. "Malfaek, our lord and saviour," he bellowed. "This is the hundredth offer, as decreed. This is our final donation to you, the King of the Dark Depths. And in doing so, we ask that you give us the gift that only you can give. We beseech you. Please, grant us absolution from death. Release us from its icy grip and allow us to live ever onwards, where we can offer many more morsels for your boundless appetite."

Xavier signalled to his minions, a slashing of his hand over his throat, which Jessalyn always considered a little ghoulish, but the rather grandiloquent Xavier did enjoy a show.

The offering began to struggle, but the minions clung on, and he soon lost strength and seemed to slump, his gait languid as if in defeat. The underlings hauled his near lifeless body towards the firepit and cast him into the flames. The drop, Jessalyn knew from experience having seen it unlit in the past, was many metres deep. The man plunged downward, and his screams filled the cavern. The air became pungent with the aroma of sizzling flesh, causing her nose to wrinkle in distaste. She and the others fidgeted while the man thrashed about in the fire, but his ministrations dwindled, until they slowed, and then stopped. Finally, his voice gave out, and the flames consumed him, body and soul, until he was nothing more than billowed smoke and the scent of cooked flesh.

"Hear us, oh, Malfaek the Glorious," beseeched Xavier, whose hands had never lowered. "As we offer this flesh to you. Grant us what is owed. And in your honour, we shall continue to bring you souls, forevermore!"

Jessalyn waited, her heart beating like a drum in her chest. The tension lifted in the cavern, even as the odour of burnt flesh became faint and the memory of the offering's screams faded. Time seemed to stretch ever onwards in the gloom, while the flames of the firepit frolicked and cavorted without a care for the strange rituals taken place around them.

And still, they waited. Jessalyn glanced at her nearest neighbours, trying to gauge their emotions to see if they were the same as hers. What she saw in them reflected her own inner impatience. The ritual was complete, she thought, the irritation creeping over her hidden face, so where was Malfaek? The other members of the Order squirmed and glanced from left to right until all eyes found Xavier. His arms had stayed aloft for many minutes, and the strain of holding them as such was starting to take its toll. His upraised limbs trembled with the exertion, until he could take no more, and he let them fall.

Xavier's shoulders collapsed and a murmur passed through the Order. He unexpectedly threw off his hood, revealing the fine handsome middle-aged features of a man who could afford good food and fine wine. His hair, although peppered with the early signs of grey, was full-bodied and slicked back, but his chiselled facial features were contorted in bafflement and his brow glistened with perspiration. He cast his gaze across the rest of the Order. Jessalyn furiously wondered whether it had all been a sham, one that she had been living for decades. She thought about the finances she had wasted, and the lives that they had so callously cast into the flames. Had it all been a trick? Had the hierophant lied?

"What did we do wrong?" asked Xavier. Gone was the pious certainty, gone was the reverence, to be replaced by a bantling's bewilderment.

Some of the others took up the question and directed it towards Xavier, but all he could do was retort with the same enquiries, back and forth, until the cavern was filled with the bathetic echoes of their endless, unanswerable demands. Jessalyn joined her voice to the others, but while she mumbled and grumbled, her ears pricked to a new sound. It came from the penumbra of the cavern.

At first, Jessalyn believed it was a trick of the expansive space, some echo resounding within the shadowy realm and coming back to sing in her ears. But when their voices all slowly died, the noise didn't dissipate. Instead, it grew more incipient, and the sound filled the cavern. The others heard and delight began to thread around the assembled. Xavier, who only a moment ago appeared sullen and petulant, now looked euphoric, his eyes sparkling with promise.

The sound continued to grow, but Jessalyn grappled to pinpoint the origin, her cerebrum struggling to make sense of it. It reminded her of the legs of a chair scraping along a wooden floor, but far vaster in volume and scope. Despite her puzzlement, her pulse continued to quicken as the noise matured, but her interest soon became disgust when the sound was joined by an ungodly stink, wafting in from the north, from the deeper parts of the cave.

One of the Order started to retch and nearly lost control of themselves as the sickening reek of decomposing flesh filled their nostrils. Jessalyn gagged and tried to fix the hood of her cloak over her nose to stop the stench. Even with the fabric over her nostrils, the noisome scent seemed to invade her senses, causing her stomach to roil. As the malodorous reek intensified, so did the abrasive grinding, battering both their ears and nose, until one, then another, finally vomited the contents of their stomachs onto the cavern floor.

Jessalyn, who still had some semblance of control over herself, realised the fabric did nothing for the smell, so she threw off her hood to get a better view of the cavern. With her vision now unimpaired, her eyes found Xavier. He stood erect and peered toward the darkened north, his attractive features bilious. His eyes were apprehensive, and his muscular frame trembled with terror.

Jessalyn followed his gaze, not truly wanting to see, but knowing that she must. They had called forth Malfaek, and now, their deity, the god of gods, had heard their call. She stared into the shadows as the most powerful of the Old Divinities came into view, but what she saw was impossible for her to comprehend. The cavern, although colossal in its diametres, bulged and strained as its dimensions groaned against the vast chitinous shell of Malfaek as he heaved his bulk into reality. His size hid his authentic appearance from her eyes, but she glimpsed devilish appendages, chthonic pincers, and two titanic, multifaceted eyes, which glittered as they regarded the meagre life that had brought him forth.

For the Order did not know his true names.

He was known throughout the universe, and the many others, across time and infinity.

Malfaek, the Dark, they called him.

Malfaek, the Lord of the Beyond.

Malfaek, the Bereaver.

He, the most hated of idols. He, the most feared of deities. He, the Sovereign of the Cold Void.

Malfaek heaved his exoskeletal mass into Gillion and with him came the ordure of a trilliard of dead, the scent of the sulphuric netherworld.

Jessalyn saw Xavier's face go white, but she barely registered his terror. Her own face blanched, as the enormity of what they had done came to bear. She heard the screams of the others as they tried to flee, but none got more than a pace or two before they joined her on their knees, facing Malfaek as the filth of his anatomy engorged within their universe.

Tears streaked down her cheeks, and she asked herself repeatedly why she didn't run, why she didn't flee that place? But she was unable to move. Her body, and that of the others, was held fast. All but Xavier were on their knees, watching with abject dread as the beast of another dimension, the prince of a dark reality, grotesquely, perversely urged himself inside the cavern and regarded the pitiful creatures that had called him from his holy slumber.

Malfaek towered above them, its insectile physique beyond their simple simian minds. The black of his shell glittered with the very essence of the cosmos itself. She saw stars, a milliard of them, reflecting off the chitin, as if he sat in the heavens.

For the longest moment, Malfaek did nothing, but then he abruptly spoke, his words appeared within their own skulls, an invasive species, ripping away memories and functions of the mind in their haste to be heard.

Mortals, you have called me. Now I am here. What do you wish of me?

The question was asked of them all, but only Xavier had the aptitude to answer as he still somehow stood upon his quaking legs. "My... my lord, Malfaek," he said, his voice feeble and teetering on the edge of madness. "We called you forth... we beseech you, release us from death... and... and we shall continue to make offers for eternity..."

Malfaek's terrible laughter occupied their heads, causing each of them to scream in agony, but the sound came from within skulls, from inside their own minds. Jessalyn sobbed, desperately trying to formulate a strategy of escape, but knowing the truth of it. There was no escape.

The laughter abruptly ceased.

Eternity? What do you know of eternity? Your lives mean nothing. If I granted this wish, you would not know what to do with it. And you speak of offerings as if the paltry pittances that you have cast my way mean anything. Why would I even notice such trivialities? I feast upon the death of whole galaxies! I banquet on the maw of apocalypse! I sate myself on the collapse of civilisations! Pah! These are but trinkets to me.

The Bereaver halted his diatribe and observed them for a time, while they trembled on their knees. For an agonising moment, Jessalyn hoped he was going to release them since he thought so little of them, but she was wrong, so terribly wrong.

Perhaps, I am being too hasty. You have given your lives to my cause, and I should thank you.

Jessalyn's heart leapt in her chest and her eyes twinkled with joy. Malfaek had taken pity on them, he was going to give them what they wanted.

Yes, I shall give you a gift. You shall come with me. Come with me to my holy plane. It is cold beyond your imagining, and the home of everlasting torment, but at least you will not face death. Come now, mortals, come with your god. We must depart. I wish to be home again. This universe vexes me.

Terror devoured Jessalyn as Malfaek repenetrated the blackness and returned the way he came. She stood, but not by her own cognisance, and followed the rest of the Order, with Xavier Watton stumbling at the helm, as they followed their god into the dark, cold blackness of the void, leaving fair Gillion behind them.

2

Automaton

Professor Sherman Clements took a step backwards to review his handiwork. He was adorned in a formerly stark white laboratory coat, now greying and dull, of middling years, with little or no hair upon his domed skull. His eyes crinkled at the corners with age and his brow was greased with grime and sweat after another hard, toiling day about his most cherished of industries, that of machinery.

Sherman sighed and wiped his forehead with his palm, further smearing the filth of metal and cogs across his waxen epidermis. He was weary, beyond even his years, having spent the last five of them labouring within his dusty, cluttered workshop. He sought what many others had failed to achieve. A thing that was whispered about from Gillion to Sogristan and back again. A concept much ruminated in the chilly cities of Ustrein. A notion heavily debated in the courts of Sadar in tundral continent to the far east. And an idea that was discussed in hushed tones even in the hovels of Memrass Nera.

His tall, slender, but stooped frame was dashed with sweat, but he felt energised now that his great work had been completed. Sherman had a noted history with mechanics, having been employed in the industry of the horseless carriage for many a decade. He had fashioned and designed many of the most sought-after transports that littered the capital, Arcton, and other parts of the world, including most notably on the continent of Ecrium, in the capital cities of Aclain and Woltensian. The Professor even had a spell with a firm that designed the vast engines of locomotives, as well as a short, albeit tumultuous, stay with the leading company for the production of dirigibles, The Gillion Airship Company.

But the transport industry and its many moving parts was not what he had spent the last five, drudging years working on. The horseless carriage, the locomotive, and the dirigible, those innovations which had propelled the Fair Isle to the forefront of the known world, would pale in comparison to what he had now created.

Sherman took a further step back, his heart pounding like the clockwork in which he so delighted in tinkering. He trembled, not with fear, but with pride. His life's work stood before him, held fast by a small network of pullies, erect and gleaming. Its body was reminiscent of a man of average height, and its torso and appendages, including its head, mimicked it so, but that was where the comparisons ceased. The machine he had created was a thing of brass, metal, and steel, with seamless contours. It was an object of clockwork, machinery, and gears. Not only was it a technical marvel, but it was entirely unique.

Professor Sherman Clements, innovator and man of science, had fashioned what he called an *automaton*.

The moment seemed to stretch ever onwards, but Sherman hesitated. He knew what he must do. To power the Automaton, he simply needed to twist the dial to provide the electricity that would bring his most cherished creation to life. It should have been his crowning achievement, something he had worked his entire life toward, but still, he wavered.

"This is *my* moment," he chided himself. "This is *my* ultimate accomplishment. So why do I dither? Why do I delay?"

The simple answer was that the magnitude of Sherman's accomplishment had not escaped him. He knew civilisation hinged on the moment, not just in Gillion, but the whole of the world. Life, created with his own gnarled hands, and forged from minerals. A new being, formed from his own intellect. That Automaton, that machine, would change everything for the indigo planet of Yuthea in the prosperous year of 4798, *forever.* He understood the enormity, had diligently worked toward it, but now the moment had arrived, he baulked. His breath laboured as his chest heaved. His heart continued its unrhythmic dance, and his armpits moistened with bodily fluids.

Sherman began to pace the laboratory. He wandered passed his worktop, littered with the tools of his trade. He meandered passed the failed attempts that lay shattered and broken upon the floor. He stormed passed the detritus of a man obsessed with his work. But with each futile loop, he came back to stand in front of his creation, in front of the Automaton, and wondered whether he should be the one to give it life.

"Am I the right man for the job?" he asked of himself. "Who am I to do such wonders?"

Yes, he had achieved much, and was well respected in Gillion and on the continent of Ecrium, but he never thought about what it might mean to his life, such as it was. He had been so consumed with that and other tasks across the sixty years of his tenure as a man of machinery that he had never stopped to *live*. He had no love, no offspring, no friends to speak of outside of passing acquaintances and colleagues of business. He had nothing to show for his hard work beyond what stood before him, awaiting the electricity that would give it life.

It occurred to Sherman that the machine of metal and gears was *his* life. There was nothing else. Abruptly, the wealth, the respect, the adoration of his peers, meant nothing to him. Perhaps it never did. He was surely never in it for the fortune, but rather the challenge. It was that which drove him forward, to keep pushing himself beyond his limits, to the far reaches of modernity and yonder.

Sherman realised the truth with a sudden jolt.

He had come to his pinnacle. Afterwards, he would have nothing to work toward. From that point, his best would be behind him. Yes, he could fine-tune his creation. Yes, he could sell it to the highest bidder, bringing wealth of such staggering heights that his former life would appear as if he was a pauper in contrast. He, Professor Sherman Clements, would be the father of automatons. The patriarch of robotics. The progenitor of artificial life. His name would be remembered for years to come and whispered through time itself. He should have been elated, fulsome even. He should have been delighted. So, why did he feel a deep foreboding dread within his soul? An existential terror that gripped his very being and sent a trembling panic down into the pit of his stomach?

Sherman, noted professor of the mechanical arts, asked himself a question that he almost dared not answer. "What will become of me and my endless grinding life and hard work and innovation if I have reached my apex?"

He would be lauded, but he knew deep down in the fibre of his being that he wasn't one for that sort of mummery. He would be more prosperous than even the most notable men and women of Gillion, but he was already rich enough for his own mind and did not crave more. His name would be discussed for decades, but he was always a shy and sullen sort who preferred his own company, despising ostentatious behaviour.

Sherman's heart began to slow, and the quivering that had taken hold of him for the last many minutes lessened. He wandered from his position near the worktop and its littering of spare parts and paraphernalia and stood before his most precious invention. The Automaton was inert and waiting. All he needed to do was add power, that electricity, and his life would change forever. It was a simple thing. He needed to do nothing more than rotate a simple knob to guarantee his celebrity. He held his life, and another's, within his own soiled hands. Hands that now did not tremble, for he knew what he must do.

He stepped forward, and for a moment the sun, cascading through the window to reflect its rays off the surface of the Automaton, blinded Sherman, causing him to blink as he raised his weary, grimy hands. But he veered away from the dial. Instead, he took hold a grey cloth and threw it over the machine. He turned his back on the Automaton, on his fame and fortune, and walked away. He traversed the laboratory, past the failures and debris, past the inventions and the novelties, but his heart, which only a moment before had slowed to a calm rhythm, began to beat anew.

Sherman stopped, not two metres from his handiwork, and turned.

"Who am I," he whispered, "to deny the life that is so tantalisingly close to fruition? Who am I to deny this thing that is already bigger than me and the whole of the Fair Isle?"

His heart thundered a steady drumbeat in his chest again. Sherman returned to stand before his construction of iron, steel, and brass, his future, his Automaton. All the ideas and ruminations that had flitted about his mind dissipated when he came to a sudden realisation. He was not going to be the man who denied artificial intelligence its chance at life.

Sherman stepped forward, his hand trembling now that the decision had been truly made, tugged the cover away, letting it slip to the dust floor, and then, without any further dithering or fanfare or introspection, turned the knob. The laboratory hummed with electricity and the many lightbulbs fizzed and dimmed as power surged down the wires and cables into the Automaton's inert body.

He paused while power pulsed into his creation's body, and with a jolt, and then a jerk, its great metal body came to life. It started with a slow lifting of its heavy arms, and a turning of its expressionless face. And then more movement, the legs, as the Automaton, with a judder, stepped from the platform.

Now that Sherman saw his design come to life, he realised he was a fool to question the decision. *Now* was the greatest moment of his time. He had become the founder of artificial life.

He watched the metal man lift its hands and stare through its glass eyes at the power it held with its grip. Sherman finally understood, standing before his creation, that he was not now a mere man, but a god, powerful enough to give life as he saw fit.

"Welcome, my child," said Professor Sherman Clements, now a deity of science. "Welcome to the world."

And he cackled as the enormity of what he had done came to life, towering over him, a thing of brass, iron, and steel, humming and throbbing with the power of technology.

The Automaton peered down at Sherman, its stare cold and uncomprehending. It lifted both of its giant metal paws, while the Professor continued his cackling, raising them to the heavens. It shuddered as electricity thrummed through its metal workings.

Upon seeing what its hands raised, Sherman ceased his amusement, his brow creasing with consternation. He opened his mouth to speak, to ask the Automaton what it was doing, but the words never departed his lips.

The Automaton's colossal metal paws crashed down onto its creators' domed skull with a moist crunch of bone and ripping skin. Professor Sherman Clements, the forebear of automation, collapsed to the ground, now broken like the many other failures that littered the floor.

The Automaton, entirely uncomprehending of what it had done, returned to peering at its now gore-spattered hands, while Sherman's lifeblood leaked from his limp body until he was no more.

3

Of Flesh and Flower

Godfrey Learmouth, a podgy yet friendly fellow, unassuming in both character and temperament, wondered why a shortcut was never just that. The instructions had seemed simple enough, and the old fellow who had relayed the information, although somewhat doddery in demeanour, had described it in such minute detail that Godfrey hadn't felt the need to question the man's veracity. But now, he wasn't so sure because he appeared to be irrevocable lost.

The pernicious city life in Arcton had taken its toll on Godfrey as of late. The incessant smog, which seemed to grow thicker by the month, the drizzling weather, and the overabundance of hurtling horseless carriages and puttering dirigibles had driven him to near apoplexy. So, he had decided to take a weekend away from the grind of the office and ventured into the beautiful Gillion countryside. That decision brought him by locomotive to the picturesque village of Easthallow. Roger, a work colleague and decent sort, had suggested it to him many months before, but Godfrey had never found the chance until now. A new business arrangement and the subsequent merger of the firm with a larger, and he had to admit, far more successful conglomerate, had taken up a vast amount of his time and energy over the previous months, leaving him morose.

Godfrey had concluded that a little respite in the countryside would do him some good and took some much-needed time off. So, he had spent a few days pottering around the village, doing nothing more than indulging in some restful walking and frequenting the local pub, The Duchess Arms, which was only a five-minute stroll from his bed and breakfast. He had partaken in an ale or two and devoured much of the local cuisine, namely the steak and kidney pies, for which the town was somewhat famous. The locals had been friendly and inviting enough, even allowing him to join in with some rather droll banter on occasion, all in good fun, of course. It was in that very establishment, on a typical Irasday, that the elderly gentlemen by the name of Mr Ellis, who had the thick accent of the region, suggested that Godfrey take a walk up to Easthallow Waterfall via the thrice damnable shortcut. The route was said to cleave through the pleasant local woodland, a few miles east of the village.

Mr Ellis had described it in such a way, and at great length, that Godfrey simply couldn't resist. With nothing else to do for the rest of the day, a brief thirty-minute hike had seemed like a perfectly sound idea. He had thanked the fellow and departed for his room. There, he had dressed in some sensible outdoor attire, walking boots, hat, warm jacket and the like, and sallied straight out in the direction the old chap had specified.

Three hours later, and he was horrible, conclusively misplaced. And to make matters worse, dusk approached, and the temperature, as it was wont to do, was on a downward trajectory.

"Damn Ellis' eyes!" cursed Godfrey, his face ruddy with anger and exercise.

The going had been easy enough at the start. Godfrey had strolled through nothing more than a pleasant coppice, over-flowing with flowers and wildlife. He had seen more than one rabbit, a great many squirrels, and one rather curious fox, who glowered at him before departing back into the foliage. But those beautiful animals had long since absconded, leaving him alone to the mounting sounds of the gloaming. What was once woodland abruptly became grasslands as far as the eye could see. There, he had expected to find the sought-for waterfall, but instead, he was met with a flat landscape, totally at odds with the surrounding hill-laden county that Easthallow inhabited. Of course, he started back the way he had tramped, assuming that he had got turned around somewhere. But somehow, and inexplicably, he must have got turned around again, as he ended up back in grassland once more. He had no idea whether it was the same area as before, or an entirely novel one, but there he stood, nonetheless.

Godfrey's jacket, although a particularly fine piece from Proctor and Hobbs, wasn't suitable for cooler climates, and neither was his simple flat cap. He had already buttoned his jacket to the neck, but now he lifted the collar so that they gave some welcome reprieve to his exposed neck. He plunged his chilly hands into his trouser pockets and peered out across the grasslands that engulfed him. The wildings were behind him, but he had ceased to believe that was the best course of action. Instead, he decided to head west.

"Yes," he said with some conviction. "That must be the way."

With a plan in mind, he began anew.

After another hour had passed, Godfrey finally saw something one hundred or so metres ahead, looming out of the black. Night had nearly fallen, and the temperature with it. The sky was garlanded with a plush carpet of stars and the moon and its cracked face, casting the area in its silver light. It would have been breathtaking if he wasn't so confoundingly mislaid.

Beyond the metres, Godfrey thought he could see a thick of bushes or some short saplings, but in the ambience of dusk, it didn't quite look right to his weary eyes. He glanced over his shoulder, but all he saw was the tall grass he had just ploughed through, so he returned his gaze to the new mystery ahead.

Godfrey's squinted assessment of the vicinity continued for a full and thorough five minutes. While he pondered what in the bloody hell he should do, he heard a curious sound on the chill breeze wafting across the field.

"Now what might that be?" he muttered.

Where before it contained nothing more than the mutter of the wind that snuck through the grasslands, it now housed the faint sound of a single, lonely bleat. He hesitated a moment longer, hoping to catch it one more time, so that he was absolutely certain of its authenticity, and not the unset of some sickness of his frozen cerebrum, but it happened again.

It was the unmistakable sound of sheep.

Godfrey stood and listened to the dim bleating as it fluttered through the stems of grass, and he found his interest was piqued. He wasn't one for adventure, and some would have possibly baulked at wandering around while the night was sinking, especially since he didn't know what was ahead, but the unassuming sound was that of lambs and cattle. And therefore, he concluded, there was no danger there.

"It's nothing more than a farm," said Godfrey firmly. "But if there is farmland, then there *has* to be people. And they will be able to set me back onto the correct path to the village."

With that conclusion sewn satisfactorily up, Godfrey eagerly started towards the sound of sheep. The distance melted away as the bleating grew in volume. In a matter of minutes, he had arrived, but what he saw before him as it materialised out of the murk didn't make any sense to his tired eyes. He stopped short, his mouth falling open, and gazed at an extraordinary sight.

That part of the county was known for its cattle production. The beef that was grown, raised, and then slaughtered was some of the finest in all of Gillion. It was often shipped across to eastern Ecrium and sometimes beyond, such was its robust and delectable taste. Bearing that in mind, Godfrey had expected to find a farm with an assortment of cattle, with a smattering of chickens and such like, but he was wrong on that front. What he saw... well, he didn't really know what he saw.

What Godfrey had mistaken as short, young saplings was metres high, heavy verdant stems. That wasn't unusual in and of itself, but it was what resided at the summit that was so startling, and evidently the source of the bleating.

"Well, I never," said Godfrey.

Upon the finial of the bizarre foliage rested sheep.

Godfrey had no idea what he could have possibly stumbled onto, but after a few pinches of his cheek and one rather hefty slap, he determined that he was, in fact, awake and what he observed was real.

The thick stems housed sheep of various sizes woven into the very summit of their vegetation, who appeared to be fast asleep. The bleating he had previously heard was coming from those... those creatures? Or were they plants? Or both? He didn't know. He had never heard of such things, and he was certain Roger hadn't seen them on his previous visit or else he surely would have informed Godfrey immediately. Either way, those extraordinary beasts were deep in slumber, emitting the occasional dreamy whine, and they didn't appear to be aware of his presence at all.

"What in Gillion is going on?" whispered Godfrey.

Unsure of what to do with himself, and since he was still terribly lost, Godfrey quietly wandered the herd. Careful not to wake the creatures, he occasionally stroked the tall stems so that he could be sure of their validity. If only he had his camera obscura upon his person. He could have taken some helios of the event and returned to the city with proof. He was certain no one would believe him, and he highly doubted he would be able to find his way back to that curious place again.

"Incredible," he mouthed. "Truly incredible."

Godfrey found his way to the centre of the herd. He lingered at the nearest stem, which contained a smaller beast, a juvenile, who shifted in its sleep and emitted a snuffling. Shaking his head in wonder, he turned his back with a mind to find a way out of the strangeness, but when he revolved, his right walking boot collided with a patch of mud on the ground, causing him to stumble back a step or two. He saved himself from falling by gripping the nearest stem, but when he straightened, he came eye to eye with a lamb.

The creature's simpleton eyes regarded Godfrey and it seemed not to care that he had rudely awoken it from its nocturnal rest, but its pupils focused and summarily widened. He let go of the stem, but it was too late as the little beast began to cry in terror. He waved his hands at it and tried to quell the creature, but it didn't stop the little terror. Instead, it seemed to intensify its caterwauling.

"Blast it all," said Godfrey, glancing from right to left.

The irksome sound continued unabated as he watched with increasing dismay the waking of the herd. It began with the jerk of heads and the flutter of eyes, but the bleating cry of danger soon traversed the field, and the sound became a cacophony of noise that was abrasive to his senses.

"I think it might be time for you to leave, Godfrey," he told himself.

He picked a direction at random and marched through the discordance of wretched creatures.

Each time he passed one of the stems, the lambs and sheep bleated louder in alarum. He would dearly have loved to stop the racket somehow, but he wouldn't have known where to begin. Instead, he just picked up the pace and strode through those verdure corridors, pushing the stems out of the way when needed.

His mindless flight continued for a short time until Godfrey felt something nip at the back of his neck.

"Blast. And blast again," hissed Godfrey, pawing at the back of his neck.

The abrupt flowering of pain and the consequent sting ground him to a sudden halt, and he glared backwards to see if he could find out where the offending discomfort originated. Above him was one of the largest beasts he had seen so far. It was an adult, pure and simple. Where before, he had observed the imbecilic gawp of lambs and sheep, now he was faced with a glower of fury.

"I'm s-sorry," said Godfrey, ashen with fear.

He took a step backwards with a mind to dash away when his cap was yanked from his head.

"Hey! Give that back!"

Godfrey swung around to find another adult with rage in their asinine eyes, munching on his expensive headwear. He nearly made a grab for his possession, even raising his hands to do so, but another of the beasts darted toward his elbow, its square teeth gnashing. He moved swift enough so that the awful creature didn't catch the skin, but it took hold of the arm of his jacket and began to nibble on the fabric.

"Get the bloody hell of me!" squeaked Godfrey, panic truly gripping him now.

His mounting dread reached its zenith, and his brain belatedly informed him that he might be in some considerable danger. He tugged his arm away from the beast, which, in turn, pulled the stem, and subsequently, the creature, toward him further still. He jostled with the stubborn animal and made some headway. He took his left hand and wrapped it around his right, which was the arm with the sheep clamped to, and pulled for all he was worth. It worked, but he had put too much strength into the manoeuvre. He stumbled backwards, straight into more of the stems. As soon as he made contact, three more sets of teeth clamp onto him. Two affixed on the material of the shoulders of his jacket. The other nipped painfully onto the skin of his left arm, compressing its teeth and claiming a deathly hold.

The monsters began to drag Godfrey backwards, while he flailed his feet around in frantic panic, kicking up dirt and muck in his wake, and cursed bloody murder.

"Get off, you wretches!" bellowed Godfrey, rather weakly. "Leave me be!"

The material of his jacket was beginning to tear, but, more importantly, the skin of his arm was also ripping. The surrounding epidermis felt moist with his own precious internal juices.

"Right," said Godfrey, firmly. "I've had just about enough of this balderdash."

Godfrey kicked and pulled his arms forward. A terrible pain jolted down his left appendage and the sound of tearing material was loud in his ears. The noise was accompanied by the bleats of those beasts of flesh and flower. He gritted his teeth and forced all his considerable middle-age weight downwards. That had the desired effect, and the fabric of his jacket finally tore. Two of the beasts were released with a violent jerk of stems, leaving the final creature with its teeth fixed on his arm. With the loss of its companions, the last of the trio didn't have the strength to fight, and, realising that its battle was lost, the beast released him. Godfrey tumbled into the muck, where he swiftly rolled onto his stomach.

Ignoring the agony of his left arm, Godfrey remained on the ground and pushed himself to his hands and knees. From there, he remained low and crawled through the mud and dirt. The sheep tried to nip and bite him from above, but he was far enough away that they couldn't reach him.

"Just leave me alone, you awful fiends," bellowed Godfrey from the muck.

The beasts of flesh and flower persisted with their angry bleating as he crept through the filth, creating a chthonic sound straight from a feverish nightmare. He continued his frenetic flight, scrabbling through the dirt, entirely ruining his fine suit, until he burst out of the herd and back into the moon-illumined grassland.

Godfrey stood and stumbled a few paces away, where he halted and turned back to face his erstwhile adversary. The tall stems and their vicious fleshy flowers rocked and swayed as they sent a shower of sound in his direction. The noise was something terrible to behold, but they were caught fast by their bizarre anatomy. He was safe. But that didn't mean he wanted to stay there any longer than he needed to.

"I've had quite enough of this," grumbled Godfrey, and turned tail and ran.

4

Madam Mistre of Marnmouth Bay

Elizabeth, of the famous family Beale, one of the foremost innovators and manufacturers of horseless carriages that unceasingly cluttered the cobbled streets of Arcton, braced herself against the biting winds of Marnmouth Bay. It was a littoral settlement, largely bereft of visitors, and wholly out of season. It was deep into the dark recesses of the winter month of Enir, in the furthest reaches of the north of the Fair Isle, many miles away from the capital and its industry and business.

The winds were brisk and laden with frigid moisture. The night was silent but for the occasional squawk of the seagulls that roamed the coastlines for morsels and to bedevil the patrons of the town. Elizabeth tightened her shawl, clasping the hems with numb fingers, gripping for dear life. She was buffeted by the gales that burst forth from the choppy Gillion Strait, splashing her face with foamy fret.

It had been many a year since Elizabeth ventured north and many more since she had indulged in the frozen season. Usually, she would have frequented the south of Aclain or the coast of Eskana with her suitor, Wilford Crowle, but he knew nothing of her trip, nor would he. He disapproved of such superstitious nonsense, as he described it. He was a simple man with simple tastes and knew nothing of the occult, but that suited her perfectly well since her reason for being in Marnmouth Bay concerned him. Her jaunt was for her alone, and although it was an excursion she hadn't made for a decade, since the year of 4788, she found that her stomach tingled with the sheer thrill of it.

And why did the heiress to one of the most delicious fortunes of Gillion find herself in the cold north on an unassuming Ebrisday? Why did she dash along a slippery street, the ground glittering with the verglas of winter? She had come to the small seaside town to pay a visit to that most revered of clairvoyants, the infamous, the world-acclaimed, and, in some circles, notorious, Madam Mistre.

Elizabeth's pulse skipped when she saw the home of the Madam. The innocuous one-story building had the bearing of a vacant shack with peeling paint and a languid gait, but it housed the greatest fortune-teller that side of Sogristan, where such things were revered. As for why the Madam had decided to live in such a town, far from the pomp and circumstance of civilised life, was anyone's guess. No one had ever had the resolve to ask, nor would they ever. No, those who patronised her abode did so for one purpose. They came to pay homage and ask that most pressing questions: *What does the future hold?*

For Elizabeth, as she dashed towards the Madam's home, skipping over whitening puddles in her exquisite shoes, obtained from Proctor and Hobbs, of course, was at a crossroads in her life. The family fortune would soon be thrust upon her young shoulders. Her father, the esteemed Mr Garfield

Beale, and patriarch of the family, was in poor health. She was soon to take the reins of the business. Of course, she was the perfect candidate for the role, as she knew her own mind and understood the finer points of the horseless carriage industry, having served under her father for most of her life. She did not fear the commitment, nor doubt her own intellect. No, she had other, baser anxieties she wished to clear up that day, rather than wait another a year or two before it was too late.

Elizabeth rushed to the door and splashed through one final, slush-laden puddle, soaking her boot right up to the ankle and almost certainly destroying the suede. She climbed upon the step, raised her numb fingers, and clasped the door knocker. It was a devilish-looking monstrosity, wrought from iron and shaped like the visage of some horned deity with crimson-painted eyes and the demeanour of a fiend. She gripped it in her frozen palm and knocked once, twice, and then finally, thrice. The clangour rattled the splintered wooden doorframe, showering her with dust that rained down from the jamb.

Elizabeth waited a moment while the echoes subsided. As far as anyone was aware, the celebrated mystic had never left her home in Marnmouth Bay, or so the rumours claimed. Elizabeth believed such tales, but that was because she had been there before, many years ago, in her late teenage years.

During a moist and sweltering summer, her family had come to enjoy the cooler winds that blew from Ustrein in the north of Ecrium and, more importantly, to escape the reek of Arcton. On a whim, while her father and mother were strolling the Marnmouth Promenade, Elizabth happened upon a gentleman by the name of Mr Burton Steen, whom she was familiar. Burton had burst from the abode of the Madam, his face deathly pale, but with a grin etched upon his striking features. Such was his delight they nearly collided, startling them both, and causing Elizabeth to nearly drop the sticky candied apple she had procured from a vendor not a moment before. When Burton realised who she was, he grew sheepish, as though caught in an uncouth act.

Due to his embarrassment, and possibly to avoid any confusion as to why he was there since rumours of indiscretion - he was a married man - often began thus, he briefly explained to her why he patronised the strange dwelling. He then said his farewells and dashed away for the next locomotive to the capital.

Elizabeth, being young and impetuous, decided to see what all the fuss was about and entered through the still ajar door after disposing of her half-eaten sweet treat into a wastebasket. What she spoke to the Madam about she had never discussed again, not even to her father, who had wondered on her whereabouts for the previous hour while she was busy with the dark arts. Whatever was said, many years later, it had come to fruition, thereby solidifying her belief in clairvoyance and the Madam's powers.

And now Elizabeth had returned, nearly ten years elapsing in the interim, with another pressing matter. She stood on the doorstep, trembling with the cold, under a cloud-laden night sky, and considered knocking once more. She even lifted her hands to do so, but the door groaned open a crack. She waited a breathless second to see if the frame opened further, or to be greeted by someone from within the shadowy interior, but when no one was forthcoming, she pushed the door and entered.

Elizabeth walked into the home of Madam Mistre, the most renowned of oracles north of Taldreel, where such things were unremarkable and existed on every dusty corner of the capital, Memrass Nera. She closed the door behind her and took a moment to adjust to the gloom. The interior was lit by a plethora of puttering candles that littered every piece of furniture throughout the room. There were no gas lamps or sconces on the walls. The candles were the only meagre mode of illumination, but what they revealed caused her heart to flutter.

The years might have aged Elizabeth, but her memory of her previous visit was still fresh. What she saw before her was almost precisely as she recollected it. The one-story building was but one room, where all the trappings of life had been scattered. That was where the Madam ate, slept, cooked, and washed. Her unkempt bed, with its four posters and velvet drapes, dominated one corner, while a dusty brass bath inhabited the other. The kitchen, and that term could be labelled loosely, was nothing more than a stove, with a narrow wooden table next to it, pushed right up to the fixings. The surface was covered in all manner of outlandish items, the meaning and authenticity Elizabeth wouldn't have dared to guess.

Madam Mistre waited in her usual place, sitting behind a small round table adorned with a purple cloth inscribed in a peculiar tongue that pained Elizabeth's eyes if she gazed too long upon them. On the table, the Madam had already laid three cards, facedown, their portentous faces obscured. The mystic waited, her head festooned with the sparkling silver turban of her order, and her body wrapped in a great fur, which was said to have been gifted to her by a Broivanian potentate. Her hands, which both rested on the table, glittered with a cornucopia of golden rings, each encrusted with precious stones.

A chair awaited Elizabeth.

She traversed the murky room and sat upon it. Her nose

prickly with the scent of the candles and something else, a hint of the sulphur hidden within the pungency. Her pulse skittered, and her heart clanged a dull thump in her chest. Whereas before she was frozen nearly to the bone, now she found she was uncomfortably hot within the stifling ambience. She didn't want to remove her shawl, as though it had become a comforting and protective blanket, so she held it tightly clasped around her.

Madam Mistre peered over the table. So far, she hadn't moved or spoken a word of greeting, but she needn't indulge in such frivolities as she harboured no surprise at Elizabeth's arrival. The Madam's wrinkled face broke into a grin. Her complexion was wan, as though she had recently been unwell, which, of course, wasn't true. She had piercing dark eyes, accentuated by the kohl she had slashed underneath. Elizabeth, battling the revulsion upon seeing the Madam's yellowing and blackened teeth, returned the gesture with a weak smile of her own. The Madam had the appearance of the ancient, but according to the legends that had sprouted up around her over the years, she had looked just so for many decades. Some said, even longer than that.

"Greetings, my child," said Madam Mistre, her voice was strong despite her age. "I have expected you." Her accent was thick to Elizabeth's ears, but she couldn't place it.

"Thank you, Madam," muttered Elizabeth, "I have come again, as predicted, to ask another question of you."

Madam Mistre smiled at that, a leering thing, and tapped one of her fingers on the table. "Yes, my child," she whispered, her dark eyes twinkling, "as I knew you would. The question you asked of me then was a child's enquiry, but now I see that you are a woman grown and wish of me something of a more mature nature." Elizabeth nodded her head, fumbling for the correct words, but the Madam interjected. "You wish to know of Wilford's intentions, do you not?"

Elizabeth, although startled by the Madam's curious foresight, forged on. "Yes, he seems like a perfect gentleman, but he..." She slowed a moment, but summarily found her voice and her resolve. "Well, he enjoys a drink on occasion, which I have no issue with, but I've heard rumours that he partakes in some of the more degenerate nightly pastimes. Gambling dens, illicit dives, whoring and such like, but when I confronted him about the matter, he denied it. I believe I love the man, and he can be very sweet, but with my father taking ill these last few years, I wish to be sure of his intentions. I will run the family business soon and need no distractions or hangers-on." She took a hasty breath. "So, what I'm asking is, are Wilford's intentions pure, or is he in it for my family's fortune?"

With her question asked, Elizabeth inhaled and exhaled the fusty air.

The Madam regarded her for a short time and inclined her head. "I understand, my child," she said, her face a picture of seriousness. "The world is a dark place, and currency corrupts all. A wise question, which proves my point that you have become a strong woman with a good head for business. I will consult the cards."

Madam Mistre, with a rustling of furs, flipped the left-most card, revealing its face, and studied it for a moment. She spun the card so that Elizabeth could see. Upon it sat a maiden garmented in white atop a curious beast with the body of a horse but two black horns protruding out of its forehead, riding through a forest where the trees were adorned with variegated birds.

The Madam squinted at her in the gloom. "The Damsel," she

said, her voice lowering to meet the mood, "represents purity, but not of body, but of mind. This is you. You are pure of mind and firm of belief, but this can also indicate naivety."

She repeated the same process and exposed the next card to Elizabeth. It contained an image of a sinister snake curled upon a mountain of skulls under a glittering night sky. Just the sight of the beast caused Elizabeth to shudder.

Madam Mistre clucked her tongue and shook her head. "Ahh, the Serpent of Falsehoods," she muttered. "He represents untruth and deceit. This could be you or Wilford. He may be lying to you about his intentions, but equally, and more importantly, you may be insincere to yourself about his objectives."

Elizabeth watched the turning of the next card with bated breath. Upon its surface sat a slumbering black cat upon a cushion doused in ruby red. Compared to the other more dramatic cards, she was quite relieved to see it until she fixed her case upon the reader.

The Madam hissed, and her brow knitted, causing her wrinkled face to bundle. "The Sleeper," she said and laid a grubby finger on the very edge of the card. "This card represents sleeping designs. The cat appears stolid, but the beast is still a predator and awaits to pounce. See here." She tapped something below the cushion where a small bone poked out underneath, barely visible to those not trained to look. "This shows hidden intentions or dark designs that may or may not have already been carried out."

The Madam sat back with a huff.

A moment passed before Elizabeth dared to ask that most pressing of questions. "What does it mean, Madam?"

The illustrious Madam Mistre fixed her gaze upon Elizabeth. "It means, my child, that this man, this Wilford, lies and deceives, but not only that, he has designs for the future of a devious nature. I do not know what for sure, but I fear for you, my child. This man cannot be trusted. I would advise that you leave him immediately, or at least delay engagement until your father has passed, and then remove him from your circle of trust, thus avoiding Mr Beale any heartache and worry in his condition." She sighed. "I'm sorry, my child. You have a good heart, but this man does not love you. You will find your own way to happiness, but not with him."

"So, the rumours were true," breathed Elizabeth.

She steeled herself and wiped an angry, errant tear away from her cheek. As devastating as the news was for her, she knew what she needed to do. She would contact the family private detective. It was a drastic move that she had wished to avoid out of respect for Wilford and their relationship. But now she knew the truth, she would crush the fool. He would rue the day he crossed her.

She stood, took the offered hand of the Madam, and kissed her soiled fingers with less of the revulsion she felt when she first arrived. "Thank you, Madam," she said with genuine affection. "How can I ever repay you for this kindness?"

"Nothing, my child," replied the Madam, waving her hand in the air. "I am well-tended for, despite my outward appearance. I have all I need. Just do as I ask, and all will be well. I shall see you again in another ten years."

"I just wish..." muttered Elizabeth, but stopped and shook her head.

"Go on, child," pressed the Madam, a smile playing upon her lips. "Do not hold your tongue here. I have no time for such immaturity."

Elizabeth sighed deeply. "I just wish... I do not mean to

contradict what you have told me. It's just... I wish I could be the one to catch him in the act or to see him with my own eyes. Then I'd know for certain."

"My child," replied Madam Mistre, a grin creasing her wrinkled face. "You have become a clever young woman. It shows great wisdom that you should ask a question thusly, even to me."

The Madam dithered a moment, her eyes twinkling, and then collected the cards with a flourish before rummaging around under the table. When she returned, she carried the most outlandish instrument in her hands. A ball made of clouded glass, its nadir a square stand fashioned from a curious metal that reflected no light. The Madam placed the device upon the table.

"Now, my child," she said, her eyes still gleaming, "do you wish to see what Wilford is doing at this very moment in time?"

Elizabeth was breathless, her mind racing and her heart fluttering. Although she was bewildered by the sudden, unexpected turn of events, she found that she did want to see, but she was unsure how the strange glass ball would vacillate the need.

"Madam," said Elizabeth, sitting down again, "I do not understand, but yes. Yes, I would."

As soon as the words departed her lips, the glass ball unclouded and became entirely pellucid. At that, Elizabeth frowned and leaned forward. The Madam never removed her eyes from the young future heir of the Beale fortune.

At first nothing happened, but Elizabeth's breath caught in her throat as a blurred image materialised out of the nothingness within the ball. It took a moment to settle and focus, but then she saw him. Wilford, her betrothed, draped upon a ragged leather divan. His suit jacket was gone, and his white shirt open a button or two, revealing his hirsute chest.

As she watched, her eye agog, Wilford raised a slender, smoking pipe. He held that most disreputable of implements, and a stalwart for those who frequented the infamous, underground dens of Arcton, where Torpor was imbibed. He daintily lifted the pipe to his lips and took a long puff. When the smoke dispersed his lungs, his eyes fluttered in ecstasy, and he slumped further into the chair. So, thought Elizabeth, he really did indulge in that filthy habit. A man like that simply couldn't be trusted. The Madam was right.

As if reading her thoughts, Madam Mistre tapped the glass ball with his extensive fingernail. "Wait a moment, child," she said with a touch of sadness in her voice. "There is more to come."

Elizabeth did as she was told. The seconds slipped by until Wilford came back from the fugue of Torpor and called to someone unseen. Another moment passed, and then she approached, a den whore, scantily clad in lace. She splayed herself upon Wilford's lap, resting her naked leg on his. Upon seeing this, Elizabeth's blood grew warm.

"That awful bastard," said Elizabeth. "He has betrayed me and my family."

Elizabeth pulled her eyes from the glass ball and met the gaze of the renowned foreteller. "You were right, Madam," she said, fury still boiling in her stomach. "I was wrong to question your skills. He is false. That much is clear. I wish I could do something about it, but I'll let Peter deal with him."

"My child," whispered the Madam, her grin taking on a sinister edge, "if you so wish it, this can be dealt with now, but there is a price."

Elizabeth's blood remained hot, her skin clammy. "Do you

mean…"

Madam Mistre nodded, her face now like stone.

Elizabeth's mind raced as she glanced from the Madam to the glass ball, which housed Wilford's revolting habits and infidelity. Her sagacious nature urged her to allow Peter to ruin Wilford's reputation and leave the dark magic behind her, but the fire in her stomach, which smouldered and bubbled, would have her take her revenge.

The decision was made when Elizabeth watched Wilford slide his hand up the short dress of the den whore and kiss her neck in the same fashion he performed on an evening in their bed when he wanted to sate his male instincts. She clenched her fists together and met the Madam's eyes.

"Do it," snapped Elizabeth.

Madam Mistre's smile widened, and she peered into the glass ball. Elizabeth followed suit, her breath now short and shallow.

Wilford continued to fondle the den whore, his attention on her neck and undergarments, and not her hand, which was suddenly adorned with a slender knife that sported a curved blade. Time seemed to slow while Wilford continued his nauseating petting. The den whore, her eyes glassy and unfocused, raised the blade to Wilford's throat, and ever so gently slashed, ripping his pale flesh, and exposing the scarlet meat underneath. The viscera came soon after, gushing onto his chest and white shirt, vivid and macabre, great gouts of it, while he trembled with his final death throes.

It was all over in an instant. The glass ball became cloudy once again, and the Madam returned it to its hiding spot underneath the table.

"Now, my child," said the Madam, "I have already sent a message to Peter to clear up the mess. No word of this will hurt you or your family. Wilford will simply vanish to one of the countries of Qathana in the distant south and never be seen again."

Elizabeth, overcame with both joy and terror, kissed the fingers of the Madam again. "How can I ever repay you?"

Madam Mistre smiled, and for the first time, Elizabeth glimpsed something beyond her wrinkled facade, a deep and sinister interior, which caused her to shudder and wonder on her rash decision. For a mere moment, she was sure that the Madam's eyes shone a strange shade, a deep crimson, and the smell of sulphur that hung over the room grew stronger. But the moment passed so swiftly, that when it was over, Elizabeth wasn't sure it had happened at all.

"I will call upon you in the near future, my child," said the Madam, the ominous nature of her comment setting Elizabeth's nerves to jangling, "but for now, return to your home and set your family in order."

Elizabeth mumbled her thanks and departed the house of Madam Mistre, her final words rattling around her skull, and plunged back into the cold winter's night.

5

The Auguries of Reflection

It was said that if you gazed into a looking glass on All Fates Eve, you would see your future spouse in the reflection. So, Lester Hunniford stood before an oval mirror. Age bulged the glass at the foot, causing it to appear strangely rotund, like the sagging of old skin. He had found his way to a vacant room within a desolate abode. It was a dank and moist affair, uninhabited for many decades. His occupancy was not by his own agency, but by means of a juvenile wager, one which he couldn't recoil from, lest he allow his mettle to be discredited.

Usually, Lester was not one for such fripperies, but the ante was thrust upon him from his most detested nemesis, the loquacious Kendall Howlande, a particularly pompous arse of a fellow. His enemy in both business and love, the bet was laid on the table over a card game where much wine had already been imbibed in full view of the most influential members of the company. He simply couldn't back down, not without being forever mocked by his peers.

So, in his hubris and pride, Lester had set forth, haughtily chartering a dirigible, and demanding that the driver not spare on the petroleum. He had departed to the raucous cheer of his colleagues with a sarcastic wave of his hand, allowing the warmth of drunkenness to fuel his temper and determination. Up into the night he had flown, watching the rain-laden clouds above as they soared across hill and dale until they arrived in the wildings beyond the capital of Gillion. He had spied his destination from the distance as loomed out of the night, and his blood had run cold, chasing his intoxication away.

So, now, Lester stood in that most horrid of places, nestled in dark woodland a few miles north of Arcton, forgotten and long forsaken: *Saint Wilona's Asylum for the Mentally Deranged.*

At one time the establishment was the finest in all the land, but now it was the home of vermin and pests. In the past, it had housed state-of-the-art machinery and the brightest minds in the field, but as things were wont to do, the economy took a nasty spill due to an eastern war in Ecrium between Sogristan and one of its vassal states, causing a minor recession throughout the northern hemisphere. The funds dried up, and the asylum went to pot, mouldering and decaying at a pace entirely unheard of before, nor since. Some claimed it was the forest reclaiming the land for its own, having never been comfortable with the presence of the asylum from its inception. Others talked of infelicitous spirits and echoes of the mental anguish that had been laid open within those dark walls. Be that as it may, the edifice, once so proud and beautiful, fell into disrepair and had been the talk of many whispered rumours and gossip of ghost stories and nightmares ever since.

Lester waited, his reflection staring back at him as if from some other, ghostly realm. He peered into his own dark eyes, glowering at himself, his spectral twin glowering defiantly back. The deformation of the glass distorted his reflection's features, but he could still make out enough to observe the greying of his temples and the pouching under his chin and around the waist. It was not that long ago, he realised, that he was a powerful man, filled with vim and vigour, but he had spent too many idle hours in the public house, drinking the evenings to their terminus.

Within the rotting structure of the asylum, Lester came to recognise that he, too, was slowly decaying, like those bitter, crumbling walls. He, too, had begun to sag and decompose. With that understanding came a little anger. He glared at his reflection, his other, with accusation in his eyes, but he was met with the same scowl from his counterpart. They scrutinised each other from different sides of the mirror, locked in a confrontation that could never be satisfied.

Lester began to wonder upon the man in the mirror. Had he lived the same life as he? Was he once unmistakably on the rise, only for it to be derailed by other, better-connected men like Kendall Howlande and those of his ilk? Lester wondered whether the ageing man in the mirror also found it easier to turn to the bottle in the evening rather than a square meal and a decent night's sleep so that he would be ready for another dreary, monotonous day at the company? Did the man in the mirror have his dreams and hopes torn from him as well?

The minutes continued to drain away until they became an hour, and Lester grew ever more frustrated. He wondered if he was a fool to have accepted the wager from a cretin like Kendall. Was he an idiot to allow his drunken self to become embroiled in stupidity? Lester frowned, causing his reflection, the man in the mirror, to crease his brow also. He scolded himself for partaking in such mummery and turned to leave, wager be damned, his reflection mimicking his disgust, when they both saw it.

From the shadows, from beyond the limits of sight, it emerged from the black, materialising from the depths, from the other side, from the recesses of the imitated world.

Bone devoid of flesh.

Skull barren of skin.

Skeleton bereft of a cadaver.

Lester and his reflection's future appeared out of the dark beyond, with a grin etched upon its ghoulish face. The phantom came to stand by their shoulder, perfectly still, and remained, staring deeply into their eyes from empty sockets.

Lester and his mirrored replication's faces became pallid with fright, for that could only mean one thing. He would not live to see his wedding day.

With certainty came terror. Lester and his echoed image fled, returning to the dirigible that awaited them on the grass, back to the world of the living, leaving the doomed behind them.

6

Through the Badlands

The locomotive whistled. Edwina came to sudden wakefulness and straightened herself, having slipped into the deep abyss of slumber an hour before. She was a native of the southwest of Gillion, the temperate coastal town of Kaldhaven to be exact, and of the sort who had been bitten by the most opulent of insects, the travel variety. She had the means to satisfy that hunger, she being of the brood of Frasier, a family of old money and even older history. Edwina adored nothing more than to see the world of Yuthea, and not just Ecrium, but the territories of Gillion's wider empire known as the isles of Westria, and the sweltering southern continent of Qathana. More recently, she had come to the north-easterly tundral continent of Etros, where, due to its position, the cold was the dominant state. That was where she found herself, on the locomotive travelling through the black on a Rhosday night, far from Gillion.

Edwina, rubbing the sleep from her eyes, peered about. The dark skin of her forehead wrinkled with irritation. Her complexion was a gift of her Esmian mother, and, although a scandal within the arrogant Frasier family at the time, casting her as the black sheep of the family, she wielded the role with obstinate pride. It also afforded her a great many freedoms to travel since the patriarch of the family, the famed and ruthless Preston Frasier, wanted her away from their business dealings.

"Not another delay," murmured Edwina.

She fished her pocket watch from her sturdy leather jacket, which matched her hardy outdoor trousers and heavy boots, for she was not one for the frilly dresses of Proctor and Hobbs. She preferred more robust garments that were better suited to the elements. She blinked as she scrutinised her battered timepiece and concluded that due to the ungodly time, it being many past the witching hour, there must be something on the tracks preventing the passage of that beast of metal and iron, as it clattered across the blackened tundra. It was not the first time there had been a delay, so she set to glowering at her reflection in the steamed window in frustration.

Edwina slipped her pocket watch back into her trousers and waited, her mind chasing away the stupor that had taken her a moment before, and listened as the great, perspiring engine slowed with a series of juddering jolts. The incessant whistle continued to announce a delay, so the rest of her carriage began to untangle themselves from their somnolence.

Time, ever the linear huntsman, progressed as it was wont to do. Edwina stood and peered out of moist windows into the black of night, not a light or sign of civilisation in sight, and waited for a conductor or another attendant. But as the minutes crept by, as the whistling ceased, as the nervous chatter of her fellow passengers reached its zenith, as a faint chill descended now that the locomotive was stationary, she came to an ominous and uncomfortable deduction.

"No one is coming," said Edwina, her face hardening.

The hulking machine of metal and ingenuity had halted, motionless, waiting, and in that most hazardous of regions, the Zomond Badlands, many miles south of the city of Xoyver. It was a devilish place, littered with eager bandits and uncouth vagabonds alike, but there were said to be other more sinister things lurking in the shadows.

"I guess I'll need to take a look," sighed Edwina.

She massaged her throbbing temples, and then fetched her revolver from her trusty leather satchel. She had seen enough of the world, its dark corners and its shadowy recesses, and had, on more than one occasion, faced dangers that most denizens of Gillion would have baulked at. During those instances, she had vowed to always keep her faithful weapon upon her person, for just such situations.

The inexperienced might wonder why she would jump to such a drastic conclusion, but Edwina, well-travelled and wily, knew the land of which they traversed. Sadar, the most notable nation in the frozen continent of Etros, was not for the faint-hearted. It was a hazardous place for the foolish and the easily frightened, but she was not one so easily alarmed.

A portly man approached her after he extricated himself from his wide-eyed family, sweating profusely despite the cold climate. "Excuse me, my dear," he said, his sing-song accent that of Otral in Ecrium. His nervous eyes briefly alight on her revolver, "do you know where we are? We were due to arrive at Xoyver at first light, and it is still many hours before dawn."

"I do not, sir," replied Edwina, her voice firm and commanding, a gift of her breeding, "but if I were you, I would arm yourself."

At that, the rotund fellow gulped. "A-arm, myself?" he whispered, his lightly tanned skin further moistened by fear.

"Against what, my dear? We don't appear to be in any danger."

"Not yet," said Edwina, putting her back to the man.

She departed her carriage, leaving her luggage safely stashed in the racks above. Her passage was marked by the mutterings of the other passengers while she searched for any attendants, but she paid them no mind. She had already concluded that they would be unable to defend themselves, being simple itinerants and businessmen and women. If things turned sour, it would be down to her and the attendants, wherever they were.

Edwina passed through the carriage and came to the next, where she was greeted with the same befuddled faces and vague questions, but she forged onward. Curiously, there appeared to be no attendants in the many carriages she passed through as she moved to the front of the locomotive. Her stomach tightened and she set her jaw. She had been endowed with a reliable intuition for danger, an exceedingly beneficial skill for one as journeyed as her, and at that moment, it apprised her that something was awry.

Edwina gripped the revolver in her hand when she came to the last carriage. There, she found a clutch of attendants, possibly all of them, huddled together in their emerald and navy uniforms. Their whispering ceased when they saw Edwina approach, and they parted as one. Upon the floor lay the driver, his more lavish uniform marking him out from the others. He, like all the attendants, had the pale complexion and dark hair of the peoples of the land, but his skin was paler by far, so wan, that Edwina quickly realised he was most recently deceased.

One of the attendants, a small, dainty woman, gestured towards the driver's neck. "Look."

Edwina knelt and inspected the offending region. The skin was shredded and broken as if some animal had bitten through the soft tissue, but strangely, it was devoid of blood. The frown which furrowed her brow deepened further. She realised with a sickening dread that the man had been depleted of his vital fluids, leaving him nothing more than a husk, a shell, of his former self.

Edwina, her face now ashen but her shoulders square, stood and turned to the attendants. "Who did this?" she asked, fixing each with a hard stare.

The petite woman pointed, her eyes wide, towards the door to the driver's position. "It came, and did this, and took the conductor, Zab, with it," she said in faltering Gillion. "It came... it came from the night..." And with that, she fell into silence, and muttered in her own language, while rubbing a wooden talisman of her culture for protection.

Edwina nodded, left the attendant and the former driver, and walked through the door.

Edwina was assaulted by a blast of icy wind. The driver's seat was empty, the engine idling down toward inactivity. The door was gone, ripped from its hinges, allowing the cold of the tundra to seep inside. She felt the frosty ambience on her cheeks, but it being the height of the summer in the month of Corasil, she knew she was in no danger from the climate. Although cold, it felt like nothing more than a wintry Gillion day, and she was attired in the correct gear for such things.

"Another sleepless night, then, Edwina," she muttered.

Edwina grasped her revolver firmly in her hand and stepped out in the Sadaran night. Above her, the night sky was awash with a cornucopia of stars, accompanied by the full moon and its fissured face. It cast its ethereal light across an ocean of long grass that swayed in the chilly breeze. The track to Xoyver cleaved through the eastern edge of the Zomond Badlands, teasing its borders, but Edwina had studied enough of the region to know that they had halted right at the edge. It was a dangerous place, by any standards, but it was calm and serene, almost like a strange daydream or a passing fancy.

She cast her eyes about and found the signs.

"There," said Edwina.

The long grass was parted where the attacker had dashed away from the locomotive, leaving a traceable path. She glanced at the engine as it steamed in the moonlight and pondered whether she should return inside and wait until the morning when they could tackle the problem in the meagre warmth of the day. But Edwina was not one for waiting, having never had much of a patient demeanour, and there was the whereabouts of the person known as Zab to contend with.

So, Edwina set forth, her revolver riveted in her hand and plunged into the tall grass. The moon lit her way. She kept the locomotive and its illuminated interior firmly behind her with more than one backward glance. Her fingers grew numb as the temperature of the metal in her hand plummeted. Despite the fear that roiled around her mind, she kept her steps even and forged on.

The minutes drained away, and Edwina considered turning back and putting that folly out of her mind, but then she found her quarry.

The even passage of tall stems suddenly gave way to a clearing where the grass had been trampled flat. Upon the ground, illumed by the cracked moon above, was a crumpled heap. In the otherworldly light, Edwina could just make out the emerald and navy raiments of the man known as Zab. She stole towards the prone conductor, fearing he had perished already, but when she drew closer, she noticed that his chest heaved with ragged breath.

Edwina, her revolver aloft, knelt next to Zab. He lay on his side, with his arm twisted underneath. His face was discoloured with a dark bruise, but his neck was intact. It appeared as if she had arrived at precisely the correct time.

"Zab," hissed Edwina. "Can you hear me?"

Zab was unconscious and unresponsive. Edwina rested her finger upon the pulse of his neck and found a weak thump. Zab was slight of figure, and after a short rumination, she reckoned that she could haul him back to the locomotive, but then she had the most peculiar of feelings. Her stomach convulsed, and her heart began to flutter. That incorporeal feeling, that intuition, which had proved her so useful in the thirty-three years of her existence, ignited. She stood, her revolver pointing into the murk, and swept her gaze around the trampled stems.

And there it stood.

At first, she couldn't believe her weary eyes. Others would have fled at such a sight, but Edwina was not one to flinch in the face of peril. The creature stood, basking in the moonlight. It appeared humanoid and could have been mistaken for a man if not for the dun complexion of its skin. Its strange epidermis was taut and revealed bulging muscles, entirely hairless, and unaffected by the cold clime. The beast was as naked as its birthing day, and stood six foot six inches tall, possibly more, easily dwarfing Edwina. Its lank black hair hung over its face, leaving only the smallest gaps, so she couldn't make out its features, but she glimpsed the gleam of razor-sharp teeth.

The fright of being confronted with such a creature caused Edwina, nomad and stout of heart, to take one step backward, but that was all.

The fiend before her was no human or animal of the day. It was a creature of the night, a citizen of the deeper territories of the witching hours. She knew she now faced death and the monstrosity had left Zab prone on the ground as bait. She had fallen straight into its awful, devilish trap. She was caught fast, but it was one-on-one, and she found those odds somewhat favourable. She regained her lost step, refilling her former spot with her firm gait, and faced the creature.

"Well, then," snapped Edwina. "Don't just stand there, you bastard. Let's have this over and done with."

She took another defiant step forward, brandishing her weapon, her finger on the trigger with a mind to unleash one swift shot, but the brute was unmoved by her demands. Instead, it stood perfectly still, like that of a statue. She eyed it then, appraising her predicament and that was when she noticed just how much taller it was than her, just how heavily built, and just how much danger she was in on that fateful night.

Edwina Frasier, the bold and intrepid explorer, indulged in a deep and melancholy sigh. "So, then," she growled, anger flaring, "I told you once already. Let us get on with this charade so that I can return to my train and be done with this."

She barked a harsh laugh and fired.

The attendants had covered the body of the driver with a white sheet and huddled in an adjacent corner and muttered amongst themselves. They had not dared stray too close to the body and whispered prayers and supplications to their deities. As an hour slipped away, they wondered on the whereabouts of the fierce woman who had defiantly set forth into the chilly night. A brave few discussed whether they should venture out themselves, but before any of their meagre plans were solidified,

Edwina returned.

It began with a rustling of the grass and the sound of footfalls, causing the attendants to shy further away. They feared the beast of the night had returned, but then she stumbled into the locomotive, causing that clustered few to gasp in astonishment. Edwina, explorer and warrior, strode into the interior supporting a blearily eyed Zab, her face sallow and glistening with spatters of a dark, viscous liquid, and her empty revolver gripped in her other hand.

She passed the senseless Zab to his overjoyed cohorts and dusted herself off. "Well," she said. "That takes care of that."

One of their number stepped forward, the girl who had spoken before. "What happened, miss?" she asked.

The others stopped and stared, and not without fear in their eyes, at that ferocious woman who had returned from the dark.

Edwina wiped her forehead with his arm and sighed deeply, before levelling her gaze upon the asker. "If I told you, you wouldn't believe me," she replied, somewhat wistfully. "We are not in danger... for now. But I suggest that you arm yourself. We must wait until the morning, until first light. Then, I believe we will be safe." She hesitated a moment, peering down at the white sheet that adorned the deceased driver. "Also," she continued after a sigh. "I would burn that body if I were you."

With her part done, she departed with a mind to find her baggage, where she kept the rest of the bullets for her revolver. The brute might not return after it had fled into the grasslands to nurse its many injuries, but she would rather be safe than sorry. She shuddered at the recent bloody work, but she cast it from her mind, firmed her jaw, and set to it.

7

Just Look at 'Em

"Just look at 'em," whispered Rollie, his voice dripping with contempt.

"Who," asked Merl, glancing about in some bewilderment. He chewed a piece of Uzroot which had already begun to blacken his lips.

Rollie rolled his eyes, sighed through his nose, and nudged his elbow into Merl's ribs, who reacted with a stifled yelp causing the root to fall out of his mouth.

"Over there, ya daft twat," hissed Rollie, nodding his chin. "Just look at them, prancing and strutting about tha place as if they own it. It boils me blood it does."

Merl peered across Bellow Street, a meandering road, one of many in the capital of Gillion, Arcton. A horseless carriage clattered past, creating an almighty din, and spraying a fair amount of filthy water off the cobbles. It was mid-morning on a Fetherday, and the day's business had long-since begun in earnest across the city. The industry of the Fair Isle never truly slept, but during the daylight hours it became a constant irksome buzz of machinery, of comings and goings, and idling dirigibles. It created the incessant, choking smog that had plagued the lesser-known and lesser-tended districts. There were many areas like the one which Merl and Rollie currently frequented. It was one of the manufacturing districts, one of hundreds, and due to the ceaseless grind of commerce, the air was already a hazy miasma that sat heavy on the chest.

Merl waited for the horseless carriage to rattle past and fixed his rather louche gaze across Bellow Street and found the source of Rollie's contumely attention.

"Who, them?" asked Merl, quite mystified. He maintained his confused state by drinking liquor, much and often, whenever he could get his grubby hands on it, which was most nights.

Rollie ground his teeth and nudged Merl in the ribs again, achieving a louder yelp for his efforts. "Yes, *them*, you prick," he growled. "Just look at 'em poncing and peacocking like tha own the place. I bet tha don't even know where tha are, do they?"

Merl was befuddled by another question of which he was entirely unable to locate the source, nor the vehemence, of his cohort's fury. He peered across the road again, more to show Rollie that he saw them, but still didn't understand why.

"Tha come down 'ere," continued Rollie, almost to himself, "strutting about, with that bloody shite they all seem to buy from Fucktor and Nobbs, rubbing tha finery in our noses. It's enough to make ya blood sizzle."

"I think it's called Proctor and Hobbs," replied Merl.

Rollie cuffed him on the back of his head, causing his flat cap to fall from his head into a fetid puddle of muck on the street floor.

Before Merl could protest, Rollie snapped at him again. "Yeah, I know, idiot. I said that as a jest. Don't you get it? Fucktor and

Nobbs. It's a play on words."

Merl, still baffled, reclaimed his flat cap from the sodden ground, while Rollie continued his tirade through gritted teeth.

"Tha come down 'ere, with all tha pomp and finery, rubbing it in our noses, while we live here in the stink and shit, next to the manufactories that tha own and run. We live in squaller while tha live like fuckin' kings and bastard queens, leaving us to break our backs, barely payin' us a pittance. We can't even afford a fuckin' physician nor ought, while those fuckin' bastards live it up. Don't you see, Merl, don't you understand what I'm saying? They shop in Fucktor and Nobbs, and we can't even afford new clothes. Just look at the rags we wear, all covered in grime after a night shift in the manufactory. We patch ours up while they just buy more, and more, and fuckin' more, leaving us fucked in the gutter. And now there's this bloody smog! It gets worse and worse every day. Don't you understand what I'm saying, Merl? Merl? Are you even fuckin' listening, Merl?"

Merl, startled at the use of his name on more than one occasion in quick succession, gazed at his comrade. The truth was, Merl was exhausted and dangerously close to being sober now his hipflask was empty of whisky. He wanted nothing more than to return home to his wife, have some stew, hopefully with some meat in today, have an ale and go to bed. And no number of outbursts by Rollie would change his mind on the issue.

Rollie fixed his eyes on his friend, his workmate, and his associate, and realised the truth. He saw that Merl was weary, and that because he had never been taught a thing, never had an education, that he wasn't the sharpest knife in the drawer, and that he didn't care for such talk. That wasn't to say Merl was stupid, he wasn't, but he had resigned himself to his life, and in some ways, you had to admire him for it.

Rollie sighed and slapped Merl's shoulder in a friendly manner. "Come on, then, you daft twat," he said, shoving his anger down into his stomach. "Let's go have a pint at the Cock on the way home, eh?"

At that, Merl's eyes lit up. They started towards the Prancing Cock public house, but not before Rollie lingered to glower at the finely dressed couple as they wandered the filthy cobbles of Bellow Street. One day, he thought, one day, there would be a reckoning. He knew that there would come a time when the industry stopped, when the business and commerce of Arcton would slow and even grind to a halt. And when that day came, Gillion would change, and people like him might have a chance in life.

But that thought was chaperoned by another dark rumination. That day, the one Rollie yearned for, was many years away, perhaps decades, and it burned inside him to wait that long. And as that idea dissipated, another baleful notion crept into his cerebrum. He thought of his instruments then, of his *tools* as he liked to call them. He recalled the glitter and glint of his knives. He reminisced of their sharp edges, fashioned from hours of whetstone work. He evoked the memory of their piercing tips, and what he knew they could do to the flesh. And with those nefarious concepts worming their dark way around his mind, he shuddered at the promise of the bloody work he would indulge in that night, one of many over the years, and he was satisfied that there would be less of those bastards on the streets come first light.

That thought warmed Rollie's belly as he turned his back on the well-dressed couple, them and all the others with their fashionable suits and delicate dresses, and fell in step with Merl, who had found a renewed focus now that there was a promise of ale in his very near future.

8

The Beauty of Argyria

The clangour of many feet sang out on the wet cobbled streets of Arcton. It had been many a year since Oscar had seen so much joviality. He and his companion made their way through the seething throng, accompanied by a great many pottering dirigibles in the sky above, crisscrossing the city on business.

The infamous artist in question hadn't been to Arcton for more than a decade. His arrival and subsequent announcement of a show to be held in the world-famous National Gallery of Gillion had sent the nation into a wild, obstreperous uproar. The papers, including the widely respected Gillion Post and The Arcton Gazette, where before had been sequestered with talk of a sudden spate of mergers and bankruptcies, were now awash with speculation that had been going on for weeks, even months, about what the exhibition might entail.

Oscar had never been one for mummery, and he certainly was not one for art, but even he had become drawn into the excitement. It wasn't that he didn't have an appreciation for the creative mysteries. On the contrary, he used to dabble in watercolours when he was a youth, but in those days, he had time aplenty to waste frivolously on such extravagances. But not any longer. He was a man of industry, and his job at Braithwaite's afforded him some luxuries in the compartment of finance. Subsequently, he had long since departed his dilapidated family home and purchased one of his own with a mind to fill it with the sound of playing children. He was still working on that grand design, much to the dismay of his mother and disapproval of his father.

Oscar planned to cement his future soon. She was by his side, gaily strolling along the cobbled streets, her arm nestled within his. A week of torrential rain had cleared the otherwise smoggy ambience, allowing them a pleasant walk towards the National Gallery. His urbane escort for the evening was Iria Langley, of the same Langley family who owned much of the shipyards of Sudbury south of the city. There, a brisk trade could be had with Aclain across the Gillion Strait. The Langleys could trace their lineage back a thousand years and were of high-quality stock. It would have been crass of Oscar to admit, but if he married into such a family, a prosperous future would be a certitude. That's not to say his own household, the Wescotte's, wasn't a respectable sort. They could trace their lineage back a good few hundred years and were in good standing with most of the higher houses. It was just that his family had been through some lean years in recent times, which he was diligently working to rectify, although when compared to Iria's brood, they were but peasants.

Iria was a fine example of their breeding. She was tall and slender with the pale skin of one who hadn't worked outdoors in her life. She sauntered with a perfect gait, her head raised high and her shoulders square. Her golden locks were arranged so they sat on the top of her head, the hair plastered straight and close to the skull, culminating in a wild bunch of curled strands, fastened together by a silver device in the fashion of the times. Her exquisite indigo ball gown, which stretched down to her angles, revealed no flesh, except that of her hands and head.

Iria looked radiant, but if Oscar could have been so bold, he thought he looked rather fetching himself, besuited in a stylish navy tweed three-piece from Proctor and Hobbs. He had left his head bare for the occasion and applied some wax to his dark hair and thin moustache. The rest of his face had been expertly shaved at Tomley's that very morning and there wasn't a single bristle to be found. He had donned his most exquisite dress shoes, also purchased from Proctor and Hobbs, of course, and a silver pocket watch from the jewellers on Steadford Street. In short, he firmly believed he looked every bit as extravagant as his delightful escort.

Blue and silver. They both sported those hues, but that was by request. The proviso of their attendance that Withday night was that they wear something in a shade of blue and adorn themselves in something of the precious metal silver. As for why, it was never explained, but Oscar was sure it would have some bearing upon the show. They would soon find out.

The crowds were thick as they sauntered along Bloomfield Way and turned onto De Clare Boulevard. The city was inundated with sounds of laughter and merriment. The cracked moon hung heavy, casting its light across the capital, revealing the masses that churned through the streets. Oscar's eyes greedily drank in a sea of indigo, navy, cobalt, azure, and in a few cases, turquoise, which he was sure wasn't quite appropriate, but he expected it would be allowed, given the circumstances. He felt as if he was walking amongst the very undulating waves of the Atlas Sea itself.

The cost of the tickets for the event had been astronomical, but Iria had wanted to go, and Oscar wasn't going to be the one to deny her. Of course, Iria could have come by her own cognisance, but he wouldn't hear of it. It cost him a pretty penny, but it was worth it to see the giddiness in her eyes when he picked her up in his chauffeured horseless carriage. She hadn't stopped talking about the show for the entire journey, while they sat and drank champagne. Her enthusiasm had buoyed him ever since, and now he saw the rest of Arcton was so impassioned about the event, he found that he, too, was thrilled to be part of it.

"Oh, Oscar," exclaimed Iria, gripping his arm and breaking him from his nomadic thoughts. "What do you think Dr Vemrarin will concoct tonight? There's so much secrecy around the show that I haven't been able to squeeze out so much as a peep from anyone. Those that do know seem to have been sworn to silence, and no amount of bribery and threats will open their lips. It's just all so wonderfully delicious, isn't it?"

"Iria, my dear," replied Oscar, "your enthusiasm for this endeavour is positively intoxicating. I don't believe you've ever looked more resplendent as you do tonight. As for what the good doctor has up his sleeve, I'm quite sure I have no idea. This is your domain. I've never been one for the arts, you know that."

"Oh, pish, Oscar," said Iria, lightly slapping his arm. "You enjoyed our last visit to the Gallery when we came to see the preeminent sculptor, Brynlee Grovese. Her stonework was a wonder, and I hope you aren't going to tell me otherwise or I shall be rather put out."

Sensing disaster, Oscar swiftly moved to appease her, but in truth, he could barely remember the event that took place a year before. He recalled telling a colleague of his at work the following week that it was a rather drab affair and not to his tastes, but other than that, it was all quite nebulous to him. But it wouldn't have done for him to set the evening off on the wrong foot.

"Yes, you're right, my dear," he said. "I remember it now. Such wonderful work. Very lifelike."

Iria peered at him for a moment, her eyes narrowing, possibly to be sure that he wasn't mocking her, before nodding her head. She extracted a slender Tanner cigarette from her purse and placed it in a holder. She lifted it to her lips and waited for Oscar to light the tip with his silver lighter. The smoking of cigarettes was a little uncouth for him. He preferred to stick to pipes when he was in the mood, which was rare, but cigarettes, especially that particular brand, were all the rage in the Fair Isle at the time.

They followed the throng along the leafy road of De Clare Boulevard and added their voices to the chatter of the night. They indulged in mindless gossip of other households and the comings and goings of the city. Soaring dirigibles bobbed and weaved above their heads, bringing back some of the smog the weather had only just cleared. There had been a few significant mergers following a spate of curious hush-hush deaths amongst families of good standing in recent times that had set Arcton to wild speculation about bursting bubbles, recessions and such like, but Oscar personally believed it was just nonsense so that the papers could write about something. They had been filled with rumours for months. That was until Dr Vemrarin had decided that he was coming back to Gillion.

It had been many years since Vemrarin had come to the Fair Isle. He last visited the capital in the year of 4772 during that ghastly upheaval with the western Ecrium country of Bredor in the Gillion Strait over certain opaque fishing rights. The Doctor was alleged to originate from somewhere in that continent, one of the states towards the east near Woltensian, although Oscar couldn't quite recollect where, as he moved around so frequently in those days. He had recently read that Vemrarin had spent some years in Taldreel, in that sweltering city of Memrass Nera. As if that wasn't scandalous enough, the Doctor had been to other cities even further south, to Dasta and Letol, and even in the tundral, northern continent of Etros to the east beyond Ecrium, to Sheyh Scijan, but much of the talk seemed to be little more than gossip and blather.

Such reports followed the Doctor. Some said he was old beyond his appearance and that he had been wandering the world of Yuthea for thousands of years. How such nonsense came about, Oscar hadn't the faintest idea, but whether he believed them or not, it was said that there was a record of man that sounded peculiarly like Dr Vemrarin from the ancient country of Sadar. The tale told of perverse experiments and heathen practices, all conducted in a language that has never been heard before or since. Of course, such things were beneath Oscar, and he didn't pay them any mind.

Despite, or possible because of the gossip, Vemrarin's performances proceeded him. Some described him as a mentalist, while others called him a charlatan. In certain circles, they referred to him as a sorcerer of the dark arts, both in negative and positive lights. In others, he was simply what Oscar believed him to be, a much-celebrated artist who had produced such innovative works that always, without fail, set the globe all a titter.

The last time Vemrarin came to their shores he brought a

strange creature from the far north of Ustrein, a hirsute, hulking beast that appeared to be nothing more than a wild animal until it spoke in accented but legible Gillion. Another time in the west Ecrium coastal principality of Eskana, he painted the whole city crimson overnight while the populace slumbered. In the Broivanian capital of Aprurg, he exhumed the inhabitants of a rather large cemetery and arranged them as if they were at a party of the dead. Apparently, the fetid aroma was appalling.

All in all, the Doctor was an eccentric sort, who always put on an unforgettable performance, so Arcton was in for a treat, but as always, everyone knew little more than nothing about what the show might entail. That was Vemrarin's way. Oscar, Iria, and the other guests were simply instructed to wear raiment's in a hue of blue and to adorn something made from silver and to arrive at 8 pm sharp. The only other snippet of information they were given was the name of the show, *The Beauty of Argyria*, but Oscar didn't have the foggiest notion what that meant as he was unfamiliar with the word or place. He could only assume that it was the name of the land Vemrarin had recently patronised, subsequently influencing the exhibition.

"Oh, Oscar," cried Iria. "We're here! Look at the National Gallery! What a sight!"

Oscar followed her pointed finger and found the source of her excitement. The National Gallery of Gillion was a mere half-mile away. The structure had built in the early days of the boom of Arcton, following the maritime expansion of the nation into the known world. With spices and precious metals pilfered from the scattered islands of Westria came wealth. With affluence came the need to build and shape the city into the decorous capital it was known for. The National Gallery was one of the first to be constructed, along with the Gillion Houses of Parliament and The Grand Palace of the House of De Clare, where her august majesty, Duchess Genevieve, resided.

"You're correct, my dear," replied Oscar. "What a sight, indeed. Wonderful, quite wonderful."

Oscar had always loved the old National Gallery, with its towering façade hewn from Westrian marble and northern Gillion stone. It was fashioned in the style of the times and based on the ancient structure of the countries of the Meshil Sea, which sat in the south of the continent of Ecrium and spilt into the Equatorial Ocean. The Gallery mimicked that style with its pillar frontage and ample windows. Two lions of Gillion were stationed at the front to ward off evil spirits. Oscar had gazed upon it a great many times, but that night, it was as if he was seeing it in an entirely new light. And the word *light* was very apt. Vemrarin had replaced the fixtures of the National Gallery with navy bulbs, which, coupled with the new portable ones that he had stationed around the street and adjacent buildings, had wholly changed the flaxen hues of the structure, replacing it with a deep cobalt of colour. Four banners had been hung from the rafters in shining silver to complete the awe-inspiring sight.

"Just look at what he's done, Oscar," said Iria, motioning towards the blue face of the building. "The Gallery has never looked so beautiful. Don't you think?"

"He's really outdone himself, my dear," replied Oscar, nodding his head firmly to show he agreed. "And just look at the crowd leading up towards the building. We almost appear as if we're merging with the colour."

And they did. It was as if they poured from the blue-hued Gallery rather than making their way towards it. Their pace joined that of the rest of the gathering and picked up speed. All, including Oscar and Iria, were keen to get inside and see what else Vemrarin had fashioned for the rest of the evening.

They passed through the towering doors of the National Gallery into a great tumult of noise and excitement to find the interior had been treated to the same decorations. Everything was cast in an indigo light and garnished with silver drapes. The staff were attired in blue suits and boiler hats, garishly painted in silver. When they entered the staff efficiently set to work in directing them to the coatrooms, and then to the bar, where they each retrieved a glass of complimentary champagne. They were led to the expansive main hall, all cast in a navy and cobalt light.

A great many seats had been arranged to face a raised stage at the far wall which housed two objects, evenly spaced, and wholly covered by silver coverings, hiding it from their snooping eyes. As they filtered inside and found a seat near the front, one which was readily provided due to Iria's family standing, Oscar noticed a blue banner hanging on the wall above the stage.

And on it, written in a tight silver script, was the quote:

If the soul had a colour, it would be blue.
Giagro, 202

Although Oscar was aware of the legendary, and possibly mythical, warrior philosopher, Giagro, he had never seen that particular quote.

"Do you know of Giagro, Oscar?" asked Iria. "I'm afraid I've never heard the name."

"I do," replied Oscar, having studied the man as a youth he was happy to hold forth. "Giagro was said to have lived in

Naptriule in the obscure period at the beginning of the New Era, nearly five thousand years ago. The story goes that he was a skilled fighter who wielded both sword and bow. He slew his way around ancient Naptriule and sold his skills to the highest bidder for whatever war might have been taking place between the states at the time, which were many."

"How very grisly," tittered Iria.

"Quite," continued Oscar, enjoying imparting his knowledge. "When he wasn't plying his expertise, he wrote a great many tales about his exploits, which wasn't unusual, but what made him stand out was he wove philosophical concepts and ideas throughout the stories. They usually involved discussions about the immensity of the cosmos and why it was a cold and unyielding place, brutal, unforgiving, and unknowable. His ideology allowed Giagro to absolve himself for his many sins as he believed that it was the way of the universe, and therefore, people were free to do as they so willed, as long as they believed it was a worthy cause. For him, it was war and death."

It was an interesting concept and one Oscar, and a great many other young men, indulged during his wild youth. A likely excuse for any debauchery.

Since they sat down the exhilaration in the National Gallery had swelled. Abruptly, the lights went out, plunging everything into semi-darkness. All except the stage, which was the sole source of light, one blue beam fixated on the centre. The sound of the twittering throng was soon replaced with giddy whispering, which seemed to ripple from back to front and back again like an unruly wave on the cold Gillon Strait. That abrasive murmuring continued for a time, until the sound of heavy footfalls silenced everyone. There was an intake of breath, and a strange tension threaded throughout the crowd.

The footsteps became louder until they changed from the sound of shoes on the floor to the wood of the stage. The tension lifted again, and there was an audible gasp from many in the crowd as the infamous artist, mentalist, and possibly sorcerer, Dr Montgomery Vemrarin, stepped into the light.

Oscar had seen the Doctor in the papers many times, but never in the flesh. Under the unusual lighting, Vemrarin appeared positively outlandish. The Doctor stood tall and erect in a dark suit, glowering into the crowd. His thick dark beard stood out sharply in the odd light, but Oscar's eyes were fixed on his gaunt facial features and the dark bags underneath his piercing eyes. His head was bare, housing a clutch of thick hair similar in colour to his beard. The last heliotype Oscar had seen of Vemrarin he was cleanly shaven, but clearly, he had spent some time away from his barber. That's not to say he looked unkempt, but it was a shocking departure from his usual look.

But what struck Oscar about Vemrarin was his eyes. He glared out into the seated gathered as if in a challenge. It was as though they had offended him somehow, and Vemrarin hadn't forgiven them yet for the slight, whatever it might have been. The Doctor stood with his arms clasped behind his back, like that of a school headmaster, and cast his intense focus around the room. His roving eyes caused Oscar to shudder, but he wasn't alone, as Iria's hand found his own, squeezing it for comfort. The room, which until a moment ago was near stifling with body heat, seemed to plummet in temperature, leaving a faint chill. Inexplicably, Oscar smelt a faint odour of rotten eggs on the air.

Vemrarin's squinted assessment of the crowd continued unabated, but then ended when he spoke. Much to Oscar's surprise, the doctor's voice was quite hoarse and rasping. His accent tinged his pronouncing of the tongue of Gillion with a strange lilt. He minutely leant forward when he spoke, but his arms never left his back.

"Thank you for coming here this evening," began Vemrarin. "As you well know, I prefer to let my work speak for itself, but this evening, I shall explain a little of my inspiration. I have prepared for tonight for many years. *Twenty*, in fact."

That caused a minor ripple of excitement, which Vemrarin silenced with a scowling stare and a jutted chin.

"I was in Naptriule during the Winter Civil War," he continued. "I happened upon the quote that you see behind me now. At the time, it meant little to me, but for those many weeks that I spent in that country, I immersed myself in the filth of war. It was my wish at the time to understand the rapacity of bloodshed for another piece that I was working on, a long-abandoned project. As I travelled the war-torn country, I saw much in the way of violence and death, before, during, and after. I witnessed the mass graves. I beheld the burned villages and towns. I observed the far-away look in the eyes of the recently fallen. But during those winter months, the coldest on record, which has since never been equalled in the temperate domain around the Meshil Sea, I beheld something quite extraordinary."

The Doctor paused for dramatic effect. Excited chatter crested but swiftly died. A strange foreboding came over Oscar. All that talk of war was distasteful.

"As the cold, freezing temperatures descended on the unburied dead," resumed Vemrarin. "I walked the moribund fields of mortality and saw something that stirred me. Due to those terrible temperatures, the colour of the skin of the recent dead was revealed to my weary eyes. In that simple metamorphosis, I saw something. I saw *beauty*. This was when I remembered what Giagro had said. It struck me as if like a bolt of lightning, literally sending a jolt through me."

At that, the crowd muttered uncomfortably, but Vemrarin seemed not to care or notice.

"At first," said the Doctor, silencing any lingering murmurs. "I believed it was the dead I was there to see, but I came to realise my mistake. It wasn't death, but that hue, that shade of colour. The colour of our souls, seeping out after death. I wanted to recreate it. Death, as you know, is too final, too infinite. Eventually, those recently perished would rot, decompose, and return to the mud, taking their wonderfully coloured skin with them. And *that* is something I couldn't abide."

Vemrarin paused again and took a breath.

"I immediately wanted to replicate what I had seen in those killing fields. It occurred to me that I could simply paint my subjects, but when I tried, I could never quite get the shade correct. I visited many morgues and used real-life examples, but the variation was myriad. I grew frustrated with the project, and nearly resigned the task, but as luck would have it, I stumbled upon the solution while researching another project in a brief visit to Memrass Nera. There, I found a treatise on alchemy that was thought lost. In it, I found much in the way of myth and nonsense, but one concept startled me to attention."

Vemrarin briefly surveyed the silent crowd.

"Colloquial silver," he suddenly said after a short silence, which caused one or two in the crowd to jump. "The process of imbibing small quantities of the metal with food and liquid for the betterment of one's health. Now, I'm not here to hawk an elixir as I've never been able to find the truth of its so-called salubrious benefits, but what it yielded was an unexpected side effect. That of *Argyria.* And in this chance encounter, I had happened upon the solution to my problem."

Vemrarin ceased his lengthy diatribe and stepped back. Where before, there was only one navy light illuminating the centre of the stage, it was now switched off, and was replaced with a duo of yellow beams, bringing the two covered objects back into blinding focus. The Doctor moved to stand by the side of the nearest, where he glanced towards the left and nodded his head. The National Gallery was filled with the clangour of steel links and machinery, and the two silver coverings were lifted skyward until they were shadows in the dark of the rafters above.

Instinctively, the crowd, including Oscar, leaned forward to get a closer look. On the stage sat a duo of tall and wide metal cages, but Oscar barely noticed them because of what resided within. Each of them was sitting on a chair, naked as the day they were born, a man and a woman, their heads slumped and their postures one of slumber or possibly death.

But that wasn't what had caused the gasps and terror that were now looping through the National Gallery. No, it was the hue of their skin. Their epidermis was a sickening shade of cobalt, but not uniformly so. It seemed more profound around the stomach, the armpits, the pubis, and the eyes. As soon as the crowd registered what they were seeing, people began to rise to their feet. Oscar joined his voice with theirs as they demanded to know what was going on. "Are those people dead?" someone shouted, while another frantically wanted confirmation that they were painted and definitely alive. A few left instantly.

Before things could get entirely out of hand, Vemrarin stepped forward again and bellowed into the crowd causing everyone to fall into silent surprise.

"Behold," he boomed. "The Beauty of Argyria."

Vemrarin walked to the nearest cage and kicked the metal

bars. The sound caused the occupant, the man, to come to life. He sprang onto his feet in terror, glaring this way and that in confusion, until his eyes found the crowd. He rushed towards the bars in all his naked glory, gripping the metal, and began to babble in accented Gillion.

"Please, help us!" he begged. "Please! He's held us against our wills for twenty years! He's turned us into... he's made us into... this... this nightmare!" He scrubbed at the blue skin of his arm as if it would rub off. "Please, release us! Call the authorities! Call someone! Save us!"

Upon hearing his voice, the woman in the other cage was now on her feet and adding her voice to his pleading, but her words were in a language that was entirely unfamiliar to Oscar.

The racket continued for a few seconds or more, while the assembled watched in terror, but Vemrarin took back control of proceedings. He violently kicked the metal bars of the man's cage again, sending him scurrying away in fear, clattering over the chair as he fled.

"Enough!" shouted Vemrarin. "I told you not speak! Enough and be quiet."

Upon hearing the Doctor's words, the woman yelped and also retreated to a corner of her cage where she huddled in terror.

Now they were silent, Oscar noticed how the man and woman's ribs protruded out of their flesh, how their bones stood sharp against their blue skin. Their macilent bodies were those of the famished and the broken, nearly skeletal. Their hands, head and feet were bulbous when compared to their thin arms and legs. And stranger still, the hair on their heads and pubis was entirely white and brittle.

Just what had Vemrarin been doing to those people, and for how long, Oscar wondered? Twenty years? Twenty years of what? What tortures had they endured? Were they taken from their families? From their countries? What conditions had they been subjected to for the Doctor's art? He shuddered to think, but his first and strongest instinct was to be gone. He tried to lead Iria away, but his attempt at flight was halted when Vemrarin addressed them once again, his arms spread wide and triumphant, his face a picture of insane, grinning joy.

"Behold," repeated Vemrarin. "The Beauty of Argyria."

For a moment, nothing happened.

But slowly, ever so slowly, a smattering of applause broke out in the National Gallery. It started as one or two, but grew in volume and velocity, until it became wild, peppered with shouts and cheers. Everyone was on their feet, cheering and yelling bravo at the exultant Dr Montgomery Vemrarin, who remained with his arms outstretched as if in victory. That peculiar, faint scent of rotten eggs grew with the volume of the crowd.

Oscar's original instinct was to flee, but standing within that wild adulation, his resolve weakened. Was it all just part of the show, he questioned? Was it art?

In his bewilderment, Oscar looked to Iria and found her on her feet and violently clapping her praise. She glanced his way, meeting his eyes. She insistently nodded toward the stage. By now, the whole of the National Gallery was awash with cheers. It cascaded down all around him until it was all he could hear. He glanced from Iria to Vemrarin to the cages and back again, his mind filled with questions. Was it a show or not? If it was and he fled, he would never live it down, and he highly doubted that Iria would ever forgive him for making a scene. His name would be a laughingstock in Arcton.

Oscar struggled with the decision for a moment, but he was distracted by Iria's elbow in his ribs, prompting him to make a decision. He did the only sensible thing he could do and lifted his hands, meeting palm with palm, and joined his admiration with the others. It must have been art, after all.

9

A Vital Missive

"The most peculiar thing happened to me today," said Dewitt Wilson after a somewhat clandestine glimpse over his shoulder.

"Go on," sighed Ingrid Barbary, laying down her spectacles next to her tepid cup of coffee.

Ingrid was used to the eccentricities of her colleague in science. They had worked with each other for many a year in their workshop, labouring away over designs and technologies, working toward what they both insisted was going to be the invention of the century, one that would be revered across Gillion.

"Well," said Dewitt, hesitantly, his pale face rather more ashen than usual and his prominent forehead knotted with a frown, "you know how we've made great steps with the Difference Engine in these last few months?"

Ingrid removed her gloves, placed them by her grimy spectacles, and pushed away what she had been fiddling with on that fair Rhosday morning. The device, a devilishly complicated thing moulded from wrought metals that had been fashioned into a great many delicate cogs and gears, was a replacement for the previous contraption which had shattered during their last test run. The pair had been working on the Difference Engine for nearly a decade. Such time and luxury weren't readily available for the commoner, but they had the means via Dewitt's parents. The infamous family of Wilson, who, if you had spoken to certain furtive sources, would tell you that they made their money from the sale of weaponry, distributed throughout the continent and even beyond. If such things had been discovered by the wider populace, it would have been the talk of the papers in Arcton for months.

"Dewitt, my friend, we have much to do today, so please spit it out," said Ingrid, not kindly.

She was the older of the two by five years, but the grey streaked through her dark hair, and the lines that clustered around her eyes, led many to believe she was far older, despite her wiry frame. She was the innovation behind the operation, while her rotund, insipid colleague was the finance. Dewitt, although passable when it came to the art of science since he was educated at Saint Annette's School for the Gifted, wasn't actually gifted, but his father had the capital to get him installed into such an establishment. Ingrid, on the other hand, wasn't an alumnus of a private school, but of the public variation, and she had clawed her way out to get where she was, although it had left her quite rancorous.

"Ah, well, quite," muttered Dewitt.

He was still unused to his partner's mordacious ways. He nervously pawed a half-eaten cheese and pork sandwich that he had been nibbling at for most of the morning.

"You know how we've been running tests on the Engine?" mumbled Dewitt. "Well, I had switched the bally thing on this morning. Just to run a few diagnostics, mind you, on the logarithm output. I was expecting to give the thing a tune-up and nothing more, perhaps give it an equation or two, but when I powered the beast up from the main supply, it did something rather unusual. The screen, well..."

Ingrid, although frustrated by her cohort's mumbling ways, found that her interest had been piqued. Call it tedium, call it the aftereffects of her daily coffee, either way, she fixed her attention on the squirming Dewitt, who seemed to be struggling to get on with it. Ingrid relaxed back into her seat and peered at the Difference Engine. The device was barely bigger than a speaking telegraph, but where the handle was usually positioned on that particular machine, she and Dewitt had stationed a glass screen where the results of the equations would appear once the Engine had calculated them. That innovation alone was a rather ingenious affair, using the type of technology administered in the moving pictures, but on a much smaller scale. Of course, it was Ingrid's design, but Dewitt did love it so.

"Please continue," said Ingrid, rubbing her weary eyes.

"Ahh, yes, quite right," murmured Dewitt, his jowls glistening with the sweat of their warm workshop, which was stationed in the upmarket part of town, another gift of the Wilson family name. "When it turned the thing on, there was a missive waiting for me."

At that, Ingrid stopped tinkering with her eyelid, and peered at her associate in a bewildered fashion. "Whatever do you mean?"

Dewitt hesitated, but Ingrid waved him on. "Well, it was... well," he said, still fumbling with the correct words, "I don't know how to explain it."

"Come on, man, let's have it out," snapped Ingrid, sensing that Dewitt might have damaged the device they had spent years working on.

Dewitt gulped, and straightened somewhat, running his hand through his thinning hairline. "The missive, well, it was peculiar, and not in numericals as we've seen before."

Ingrid took further attention, albeit in a wearied manner. The Difference Engine was designed to calculate and tabulate polynomials. A few lesser devices were on the market, but most were woefully inadequate and entirely too large for the job or the expense. Ingrid and Dewitt had been working toward streamlining the machine and manufacturing it in such a way that it would be affordable for most of the businesses of the capital. So far, when it had been working correctly, it had spewed forth the necessary digits, but it had never done anything else. So, unless Dewitt had entirely lost his senses, it was quite an odd development.

"Dewitt, are you sure?" asked Ingrid, her face a picture of gravity.

"It's still there, now. I didn't dare remove it, but I haven't really got my mind around it yet. It just seems so, well, *strange*."

"And it's there now? This very instant?"

Dewitt nodded.

Ingrid stood and walked over to the Engine. The machine was bathed in the late afternoon sunshine that burst through the open window. It's brass and metal workings glinted where the glass façade reflected the light. She came to stand by the machine and found what Dewitt had been mumbling about, causing her befuddled frown to increase in intensity.

Upon the glass front was written a missive as Dewitt had so inadequately explained. The Engine had the facility to use the alphabet as well as numbers, but they hadn't programmed the machine to use them yet, so it was a great mystery to Ingrid, and one that set her heart to flickering.

Without another word, Ingrid sat down on the stool, wheeled it forward, and began to read:

Dear Reader,

I hope this message finds you intact. The year is 5002, and the war has been fought and lost. I wish I could be the one to tell you that we won, and although blood and death was bestowed on both sides, we weren't the victors. In truth, the war was lost one hundred years before, but it has taken us decades to realise that.

So, why this message?

Well, in this year, the year of our defeat, our brightest minds have created a thing that was impossible. The technology is beyond me, but I'm told it can send a message backwards, through the ages, into the past.

I know what you're thinking. That this is madness, or a joke, but you must listen. In the last years of the 50th century, the people of that era lived through a great many calamities, and it left them bereft of hope. They turned to their leaders for guidance, to democracy, but there, they found only the self-serving and the corrupt. And from that, apathy sprang forth like a spring sapling... Not that such things exist anymore, but I digress.

A void was created, a cavernous hole. The people grew exhausted by the endless bickering of the elected powers and their ability to do nothing in the face of the growing collapse of the eco-system, of the failing environment, of the increasing extinction of wildlife. So, they turned inward, toward the meagre pleasures they could eke out of their lives. And while their backs were turned, the powers-that-be bled the world dry until there wasn't enough left for anyone.

And then the fighting began.

I will not terrify you with how the battle was fought, but it was on many fronts and with new and awful technologies. Needless to say, the casualties were beyond counting, and now the world is barely more than a blistered rock, exhausted of life, and teetering on the brink of obsolescence. Some have begun to flee to the stars, but many who are left are now trapped.

Please, dear reader, please listen to this warning.

We have sent out this message back to 4878 when we believe the technology now exists to read our warning, but this machine is inexact and prone to mistakes. If this isn't that time, please pass on our message. Explain that the people need to remain engaged in democracy, and that they cannot despair, even though the temptation is so great. This message is of the utmost importance. The very continuation of life on this planet is at stake.

Please, dear reader, please do something.

You are our only hope.

Ingrid leant back in the chair and released the breath she hadn't realised she held. She couldn't process what was written as the missive was so fantastical, so unbelievable, that a mere moment after her brain digested it, she came to the conclusion it was a jest perpetuated by Dewitt or some other fool, and not becoming of a woman of science. There was no other explanation. Ingrid had always thought of Dewitt as being a bit of a gobemouche and now the notion had been proven.

Ingrid stood and turned to look at Dewitt, who was sitting and watching with wide, fearful eyes. "Is this a joke?"

"No," he squeaked in reply. "I promise you that I found the missive waiting for me when I turned the machine on. I swear on my family name that it's true."

"It simply cannot be," replied Ingrid, growing tired with the charade. "No such technology exists today. And time travel is impossible."

After a moment's pause, she continued, "And what the missive says is blatantly claptrap. Our democracy is stronger than ever in this year of 4798. And the environment? It's entirely fine. Lush and beautiful and will be for centuries to come. This, this *nonsense*, is a lie. Someone is playing silly beggars with us, man. It's probably a rival trying to derail our work. Can't you see that?"

Ingrid marched back to her chair to resume her work. She was irked at the distraction and with her colleague's lack of common sense. She set back to it, pushing the nonsense out of her mind, consigning it to some idiocy that was below her station. In some ways, it didn't surprise her that Dewitt would fall for such an obvious prank since he lacked any meaningful sense to begin with.

After a short time, which Ingrid spent tinkering with her work and Dewitt spent staring at the Difference Engine, the young fellow cleared his throat, something he occasionally did to get his partner's attention when she was in a particularly foul mood.

Ingrid raised her head, her face clouded in annoyance. "Yes, what is it?" she snapped.

Dewitt blanched. "What... what about the missive? Shouldn't we tell someone about it? Surely someone needs to know. It seems important."

"Don't be a fool, Dewitt," replied Ingrid, shaking her head like that of a disappointed teacher. "It's a jest, nothing more. Now, we have work to do. If it bothers you so much, go and delete it. I promise you what it says is lies, a joke in poor taste. Wipe it and be done with it."

Ingrid focused her attention back to the matter at hand, but out of the corner of her eye, she watched Dewitt lumber to his feet, walk to the device, fiddle with the contraption for a short time, and then return to his seat.

For many minutes, they sat in silence, but eventually, Ingrid couldn't help but purloin a glance at her colleague. She discovered him at his desk where he stared out of the window at the smoggy cityscape of Arcton, with its many dirigibles idling above, a forlorn look upon his face. Ingrid signed and returned to her work, relegating the whole affair to nonsense and frippery.

10

The Feast of Shrurosh

As he walked those filthy, limestone streets, Earnest Tabiner, a noted man of business, wondered how it was that he found himself in that most decadent metropolis of Memrass Nera, so far from Gillion, and during its most notorious festival. His business in the strange country of Taldreel was complete, but he was forced to linger like an unwanted and unlooked-for embrace. The negotiations for the merger of the company with another conglomerate following the curious death of one of their major patrons had taken far longer than he would have hoped. So long, that he had missed the last dirigible north, leaving him stranded until the celebrations concluded.

So, it seemed to Earnest his trip was both sweet and sour. The saccharine being the successful closing of the deal, and the acrid being marooned, but at least Mr Dresar had allowed him to keep his rooms at the Grand Numzir Hotel. That was a stroke of luck, as he would have been stuck without a bed for the night in a city teeming with revelry.

But as comfortable and stylish as the Numzir was, Earnest quickly grew bored with his pleasant rooms, doing nothing more than listening to ever-creaking ceiling fans, which did little or nothing for the sweltering heat of the southern hemisphere. No, he would have rather been outside. Surely, he reasoned, the festival had some redeeming qualities since it had ground the city to a standstill. The business of the conurbation was well and truly shuttered for the weekend to be replaced with merriment and debauchery. So, with no better entertainment presenting itself, Earnest ventured forth into the night.

The air was stifling, Earnest's skin seeped with perspiration. He traversed the grimy streets with their tall, enclosing walls, fashioned from the same cooling limestone as the road underfoot. The night overflowed with the citizens of the metropolis. The garb of the land had always been a mystery to him with its furtive cloaks and wrappings, although sensible for sweltering heat and blistering sun, if not a little unfashionable. But now that the city folk had donned grotesque masks in the honour of their peculiar gods, he discovered Memrass Nera had become a near terrifying labyrinth of depravity.

Food and drink flowed through the fusty streets. There was ale and hashish aplenty, and he would have been deceitful if he had said that he hadn't indulged, but it was challenging to decline when it was thrust into his hands by a Taldreelan, attired in a frightful manner, who simply wouldn't take a firm no for an answer. Sweetmeats and tart candies were everywhere and, although delicious, they left a strange insistent residue on the tongue that no amount of ale would wash away.

Earnest swiftly became a nomad, negotiating the bustling, narrow alleyways on whim and fancy. Memrass Nera had never been a handsome city in his opinion. He found the tall walls, a necessity during the hot days, rather intimidating since they produced dark corners and shadowed passageways. But the roads were so thronged with city folk, arrayed in all manner of outlandish and chthonic clothing, that he saw it in a different light.

The heat, the reek, and the rancour certainly put him on edge, but, and it may well have been the hedonist nature of the city, he found that he was rather titillated. It felt like an act of rebellion. A man of his stature, of the family Tabiner, notable for their business acumen, tramping through the dusty streets of one of the most disreputable cities in the southern hemisphere, and possibly the world? A gentleman of the Fair Isle wandering a wicked land without a chaperone, letting his feet wantonly guide him? It would be a scandal if anyone had caught wind of it.

But of course, they wouldn't, not so far away from home or within the throbbing multitude. And that was perhaps the source of Earnest's titillation. Yes, his three-piece suit, purchased from Proctor and Hobbs in Arcton, of course, was wholly unfit for such a scorching climate. He stood out like a sore thumb, especially with the locals so garishly attired as they were, but no one seemed to mind. No, in fact, they seemed to adore his attendance. They greeted him in the peculiar tongue of the land, and, although he had not the foggiest what they were saying, they seemed to be pleased to see him.

Earnest meandered past a public house overflowing with inebriated patrons. Each of them with a sloshing drink in their hands, a local delicacy in the form of a dark, bubbly ale. From the crowd, one of the locals raced toward him. The man's mask hung down around the back of his head with the straps stretched across his neck. Earnest barely had a moment to get his wits about him when the fellow gripped him painfully by the shoulder and bellowed something into his ear in the native dialect.

Of course, none of it made sense to him. Earnest had never bothered to learn the language since he usually had a translator upon his person when conducting business, but she was away that evening, somewhere in the madness.

"I'm sorry, sir," said Earnest, gesturing to his ear. "But I don't understand. Do you speak Gillion?"

The local regarded Earnest for a moment, his eyes unfocused, but then they sharpened, and a broad grin broke out upon his bristled face. "Yes, yes! I understand, my friend," said the fellow, hoarsely, and in quite legible Gillion, although with a heavy accent. "I understand many of the languages of the northern continent. It is my business to do so. I'm a *sorra*, a merchant, a trader, from the markets in the south of the city. You must have visited the emporia, no? I know that you have. A man like yourself, surely, you've journeyed there?"

"Yes, of course," said Earnest, nodding, looking for an exit from the conversation.

He had visited the southern markets many years ago, but he was in no mood for banter. It wasn't that he feared the man, but his breath, laced with alcohol and onions, was turning his stomach somewhat, and the fellow was roaring drunk to boot.

The man's eyes didn't focus for more than a few seconds, and then they set to rolling around his head, but he abruptly became serious again. "Good, good, my friend," he muttered, stifling a burp. "That is good. Memrass Nera is one of the oldest cities in the world, only rivalled by ancient Xoyver in Sadar, and everyone must visit it at least once in their life. Do you know that this city can trace its lineage back four thousand years?"

The local raised four fingers while pressing the thumb to his palm to emphasise the point. "*Four thousand.* That is a great deal of history, my friend. A great deal more than your Arcton, no?"

"Impressive," agreed Earnest half-heartedly. He glared into the crowd to see if there was room to escape. But it was packed solid and getting more crowded still as patrons seemed to be flowing out of the public house, reminiscent of an antediluvian deluge.

The man grasped Earnest's shoulder further, causing his roving eyes to lock onto his. The local was suddenly lucid again, although there was a great deal of spittle in the corner of his mouth.

"My friend, do you know of Shrurosh?" he asked in a hissed whisper.

Earnest tried to take a step back, but he was held fast.

"Shrurosh?" replied Earnest. "Isn't this his festival?"

The man cackled briefly at that, slopping his dark ale onto the dusty street. "Yes, yes, it is," he said, his face abruptly grave again. "The *Feast* of *Shrurosh*. He is one of our chief gods. He is the god of merriment, of jollity, of wine, and such like."

"Wasn't he associated with sacrifice?" asked Earnest, his curiosity getting the better of him. He had read as such in some literature on the subject at the hotel.

"In the past, maybe," said the man, shrugging. "He was the god of the games, the orepti, but that was many years ago." He tapped his chest. "To me, he is the god of merrymaking. We, the people of his land, need to let ourselves go everyone once in a while. Do you understand? This land is harsh, it is hot, and it is arid. It is a hard life here, but then this festival, the Feast of Shrurosh, happens but once a year, and this, *this* is when we enjoy ourselves, my friend. Do you understand? Whatever happens here tonight, *stays* here tonight."

The drunkard's words, although delivered rather ominously, lost their potency when he detached from Earnest's shoulder and rushed a pace or two away to vomit the contents of his stomach onto the limestone floor, much to the delight and applause of the many others around him. But the pause gave Earnest the opportunity he needed. He imbibed himself into the flowing crowd, returning to his nomadic wandering of the city.

Earnest had always known Memrass Nera to be a city of perverse whims if you were the sort who searched for them. There were hashish bars aplenty, as well as public houses for the serving of alcohol. But there were also shadier regions where the more degenerate tastes were sated. The Quarter of the Devil's Tongue, the opiate known as Torpor in Gillion, where you could purchase the fiendish remedy. The Prostitution District was another. There were also faint, near indistinct rumours of another baleful prostitution quarter where mutilation was the business of the dark hours, but he had never known anyone who frequented such places, so he didn't know the veracity of the rumours. It could well have just been simple city gossip.

Either way, the murkier portions of the populace of Memrass Nera need not fear reprimand from the dubious authorities of the city as law and order had been forsaken for decadence. Earnest observed more than one brawl, sometimes involving many people, both men and women alike. He smelt hashish and Torpor on every corner. And, of course, there was much in the way of bawdy singing and dancing.

He passed a well-lit alleyway with puttering lamps illuminating where a couple indulged in some heavy petting while a small group of elderly city folk watched impassively on, as if they were at a rather raunchy show at the theatre. It seemed that it wasn't to their tastes, as they smoked pungent dark cigarillos and talked amongst themselves in a wearied manner, only half-observing the display.

Another similarly murky ginnel produced some sort of gang warfare, with two large groups, all adorned in their festival masks, circling in each other, each gripping the curved knives of the region.

Another such snicket exposed the most peculiar puppet show where the puppeteers used life-sized dolls. Earnest slowed to watch, but his intrigue soon turned to revulsion when he released that they weren't, in fact, dolls, but city folk, tied painfully to ropes, who were being hoisted and elevated against their wills into a macabre pantomime.

The populace were not the only living creatures that visited those dark, narrow conduits. The city seemed to be infested with a great many moribund canines. The packs rushed from alley to alley, fighting over the banquet of scraps that had been dropped onto the streets by the thousands of drunken inhabitants, leaving their excrement, and in some cases their lives, behind them, before the packs moved on to fresh pickings. The dog was revered in Memrass Nera and even had a deity, Uldin. The residents left food for the creatures, as well as providing shelter, so the city teemed with them.

While Earnest navigated the strange metropolis, the night deepened. Midnight approached. Accordingly, the temperature declined somewhat, aided by the architecture of the city with its cooling limestone, but he still found his body was perspiring at an astonishing rate. In a moment of sheer revelry, he removed his suit jacket and threw it over his shoulder in a jocund manner, unbuttoning his waistcoat to reveal his damp white shirt underneath. He allowed himself a more relaxed gait. That bonhomie was further aided by an ale or two, and a short puff on a smouldering pipe of hashish a local woman thrust into his hands. With the hash and the alcohol safely in his system, he smiled a lot more and simply enjoyed the profligacy that swirled all around him like the mid-summer tempests which haunted the region.

"Yes, that drunken fellow was quite correct," muttered Earnest, a dopey smile on his face. "It is good to let your hair down once in a while."

He turned a dusty corner, one of many, and came to an expansive square that housed a belltower, illuminated from below by a bright white spotlight. The cracked waxen moon rested on the top corner as if it had been placed there by some strange design. It read a few minutes to midnight. Judging by the size of the plaza, he had come to one of the epicentres of the quarter, and it was packed with city folk accordingly. He made his way to the edge of the insanity, literally nipping at its heels as thousands of Taldreelans, who had come to see the birth of the witching hour. He moved away from the street and took a spot by a shop that sold items wrought from metals. There was space enough for him to loiter and watch the proceedings.

"Now, would you look at that," said Earnest, shaking his head in wonder.

A great wooden statue of their most revered deity, and of which the festival was named, the chimeric man-goat, Shrurosh, had been erected at the very heart of the square. The effigy loomed over the whole of the multitude, glowering with ligneous eyes. The beast was easily as tall as the belltower and fashioned in a haphazard sort of fashion, hewn with jagged edges and sharp corners, but that didn't detract from its presence. No, rather, it only added to it.

Shrurosh, the deity the drunkard had referred to, was humanoid in countenance, and reminded Earnest of Oteus, the playful god of Naptriule, who played the pipes, but only in its chimeric, goatish nature. The good-natured divinity of the Meshil Sea delighted in play and song, while that towering creature sported bulging muscle, distended claws, thick hooves, and piecing horns. There was nothing remotely mischievous about Shrurosh.

The merriment began to climax as the seconds ticked towards midnight. Earnest's eyes were for the wooden statue standing squarely in the plaza. He felt as though the great beast was staring at him, and even when he moved to another spot and stood by the window of a shop, its lifeless, wooden eyes seemed to find him, as if seeking him out.

For a dreadful moment, Earnest feared the beast wanted him gone from the city. Memrass Nera evaporated around him, taking the revellers and the debauchery with it, until it was just him and Shrurosh. The man-goat glared at him from the heights, and he took a step back against the window, where he felt the cold glass penetrate the moist material of his shirt. All sound ceased to be, and the air became chilled despite the heat of the season. The moment stretched ever onward. He grappled with his instinct to the point where fleeing became a sincere option, when the cold eyes of the effigy abruptly began to glow in a rubicund hue. The radiance became ruddier still, and Earnest's dread peaked.

"I-I don't know what's come over me," whispered Earnest, pawing at his shirt collar.

As if that wasn't terrifying enough, smoke discharged from Shrurosh's eyes, billowing upwards into the star-filled night sky.

The sight bewildered him, but Earnest's ears redelivered the sounds of the plaza to his ears. Midnight had come and a great roar been propelled toward the heavens by the rowdy city folk. Now that some of his senses had returned, his rational mind came to life. He noticed that the locals had lit the imitation, the effigy of Shrurosh, and set the enormous wooden statue on fire. The scent of it came to his nose as the square was filled with the bitter fumes of smouldering wood. He realised he was witnessing the zenith of the festival. A sacrifice, as he had stated before to the drunken local.

"Get a grip of yourself, man," snorted Earnest, straightening.

He stepped away from the cool glass of the window, scolding himself for allowing such juvenile thoughts, and proceeded to watch the chimeric deity burn to the ground. The festivities continued unabated.

Eventually, the flames consumed Shrurosh, and the statue collapsed in a great plume of sparks and smoke, much to the glee of the watchers, including Earnest, who was happy to see it gone. The Feast would continue into the night, but he wanted no further part of it. He yearned for his bed in the Numzir and its creaking ceiling fans.

He departed the plaza and returned in the direction he came, back into the blistering night with the promise of a cold bed in his mind.

As soon as Earnest began to retrace his steps his head started to swim. He had imbibed a great deal of ale, more so than was typical for him and he was unused to its robust effects. His cerebrum seemed to throb with the toxins as they wove their grip upon his grey matter. Suddenly, his legs loosened, and he stumbled through the seething crowd. Now that the witching hour had been and passed and the Feast had reached its acme, the city folk took their debauchery to new heights.

"Look at that fool," cackled someone. "His legs are leg jellied eels."

They roared with laughter as Earnest, his head lolling and his bearing unsteady, muddled past them. Some shouted obscenities at him, while others cheered his staggered progress.

"Lost, are you?" chided a woman, chortling at his plight. "Do you want me to hold your hand?"

Others berated him in their own language until it felt like the whole city laughed at him.

In that state, Earnest took a great many wrong turns until the path back to the Numzir was entirely nebulous to him. His thoughts were a miasma, and his feet, untethered by the constraints of the rational mind, led him on a merry dance through the revelry.

On and on, he reeled, blundering through the increasingly inebriated city folk. In the more pleasant regions of the city, where his fashionable hotel was housed, the locals saw him as a novelty in his fine suit, just another tourist, nothing more. But now he had stumbled into the perverse districts, the dark places of which only the initiated should tread. He was met with open hostility, although he was blind to most of it.

"Be gone!" growled someone. "Your kind are not wanted here!"

"Away," spat another. "We do not want outsiders here."

Earnest continued his bibulous roving, unaware of the dark glances and the verbal threats he endured, plunging deeper and deeper into such places where no stranger should walk.

Unbidden, he passed the prostitution district and its blackened windows, where scantily clad men and women from all junctions of Qathana stood on street corners and bellowed their fleshy wares.

Unknowing, he traversed the Quarter of the Devil's Tongue, the stench of the many smoking pipes enveloping him from the cafes and dens where greedy addicts inhaled that filthiest of drugs for their hard-earned coin.

And finally, his wanton feet brought Earnest to the clandestine region, that most awful of districts, a quarter so harrowing, so macabre, that even the citizens of Memrass Nera feared its name, keeping it secret. That awful corner of the city held no signs, was on no maps, and was never spoken about within or without polite company. Certainly, rumours flitted about the city, but they were wrong. Mutilation was not sold there, but it was a consequence. Something far worse lurked.

Earnest stumbled and fell.

When he hit the ground, his face met a puddle of reeking water, which splashed into his nose and mouth, causing him to splutter with shock. The abrupt nature of his collapse brought a sudden sobriety to him. He wobbled onto his feet from the limestone street and tottered a step or two away to lean on a wall. For a time, he just breathed deeply and let his head clear. He still felt the aftereffects of the ale and his trek, but the shock had cleared much of it.

"Where am I?" asked Earnest, peering about.

That was when he noticed the crowds had vanished. Gone was the gaiety, gone was the merriment, to be replaced with an eerie calm. The empty street held nothing more than dim gas lamps, which issued some scant light on a dusty, shadow-laden street. He put his hand to his throbbing head, cast his gaze around, and wondered what he should do. He tried to think sensibly and concluded that he should retrace his steps, but each direction looked the same as the other. He dithered on the spot, turning this way and that, his head spinning with the effort, when a sound came to his ringing ears.

"Now, what might that be?" mumbled Earnest.

Ignoring the roiling of his stomach, he strained to listen. In the deathly silence, he heard the faint roar of a crowd. It came to him atop the humid breeze from the east, away to his right, and around the corner of the street. He dawdled, but with each passing moment, the roar of a mob grew louder. It was so loud that he determined he had located the revellers, which, in turn, would lead him back to the Numzir. And, more importantly, to the safety of his bed.

"Yes, that's it, the Numzir," said Earnest firmly.

With a destination now in mind, Earnest set off, stepping carefully so as not to upset his already fragile condition. He turned the corner and found it empty, but the sound of the crowd grew in strength, affirming his mettle enough for him to continue. He passed another street, and then another, each as desolate as the other. With each step, the sound of a multitude became louder. Finally, after a few minutes of tramping, he found what he was looking for.

Before Earnest loomed the source of the racket, but rather than a merry gathering enjoying the festival, he found spectators in their thousands gathered about a deep amphitheatre. Earnest, his face wan and moist with perspiration, his expensive jacket lost somewhere on the journey, pushed through those at the edge and looked to the nadir.

Earnest had stumbled upon a place that was only whispered about. He had come across one of the largest and most depraved of fighting pits. The gladiatorial tradition, known as orepti, of which Shrurosh was famous, had been handed down for thousands of years in Taldreel, from when the country was the dominant force in the southern continent. In those days, it was slaves that were forced to battle to the death on the sands below to sate the blood lust of their god. But now only the insane and the destitute came to try their luck against the combat-hardened champions, and even then, only at certain times of the year. Namely, the Feast of Shrurosh.

Earnest didn't understand what he had found. He gazed across the many heads, past the raised fists, across the screams of bloodlust, and observed two wretched men, garbed in nothing more than loincloths and adorned with spears, clashing with a single adversary. He was as hulking brute of a man, similarly attired, but for a fiendish mask made to resemble Shrurosh. He wielded a huge axe as if it weighed nothing.

"What in the bloody hell is going on here?" said Earnest.

As he watched in growing terror, the two moribund fellows suddenly dashed as one in a pincer motion towards the hulking brute, their spears aloft. The gladiator easily sidestepped their meagre attack and severed the slowest man's head clean off. He then dove towards the other and split him asunder. Viscera splattered the sand and coated the gladiators exposed, bulging legs. He brandished his weapon in victory.

The crowd bayed and howled with delight, but Earnest had seen enough. He turned and tried to burst through the cheering crowd, putting his back to the savagery, but the city folk were thick behind him. Using some force, he tried to push his way through, but there was no give. Instead, he was met with the laughter and curses of the assembled, who shoved him backward, jostling away from the sanctuary of the quiet streets.

"Let me through! You vile beasts! Let me through," cried Earnest, the desperation coating his chin with spittle. "I do not belong here. Let me through!"

The crowd laughed evermore, and abruptly seemed to close in on him, leaving no avenue for escape. He struggled, thrashing in his terror, and struck any who would came too close, but he was trapped.

One of the multitude stepped forward and threw an empty bottle. It sailed through the air and connected with the back of his skull, causing all to turn to darkness.

When Earnest awoke, his first thought was that he was back in the Numzir, in his bed, and that he had slept through the night. He opened his eyes a crack with a mind to call reception on the speaking telegraph for some coffee and breakfast, but then the cruel howl of the crowd came to his ears and his eyes snapped open.

"No, please no," pleaded Earnest.

He languished at the base of the amphitheatre. He scrambled to his feet, causing sand to explode in all directions, but when he was upright, he saw the hulking gladiator with the visage of Shrurosh upon his head, swinging his blood-spattered axe, stalking toward him.

As the cold realisation of his predicament settled, Earnest turned to run, but every which way he looked, he was met by the howl of the throng. And a new understanding settled in his mind.

"I'm caught fast," he said, the realisation causing him to sound calm.

All the while, the brute tracked towards him, muscles swelling with each lumbering step.

Earnest took a staggering lurch backward, where his heel met something solid. A spear, the same item that the two wretched fools had fought with not a moment before. Earnest bent forward and retrieved the weapon. It felt strange in his hands, heavy, but not so much as he would have guessed. It glistened with blood and left his fingers sticky. As he peered at the metallic tip, it reflected the moonlight. He gripped it in his hands and turned towards the unsolicited foe who still stomped towards him.

Earnest had never been a fellow who indulged in fisticuffs. He was a man of business, of education, of Gillion. Such uncouth activity was beneath one such as him, but at that moment, when faced with certain death, he found a flame deep within, a burning desire to live. He held onto the notion, grasping it with all his being, and released a bellow. He charged with the spear point facing towards his uninvited nemesis.

Earnest dashed across the sand, like a jousting knight of old Gillion, kicking up grit in his wake, and made for the beast of a man who bore down upon him, his ears awash with the sounds of the roaring crowd. As that smouldering fire deep within became a burning torrent, he snarled like a beast, tapping the primal instinct for survival, urging himself to attack.

The metres disappeared as Earnest propelled himself to battle, his heart suddenly soaring with it. The thrill took him, and he grew confident, unleashing another war cry, a sound that he didn't know he could produce.

"For Gillion!" roared Earnest, for want of something better to say.

He stormed toward his adversary, and in those brief moments, he imagined winning the contestant, much to the shock and awe, and then adulation, of the astonished crowd. He would be a hero, a legend, a tale to tell children. Yes, he could win, he had to win, he must win.

The point of Earnest's spear bore down, and he sensed victory. But the brute, shining with sweat and flecked with stale viscera, whose motions had been slow and cumbersome a moment before, suddenly darted away, as swift as summer lightning.

Before Earnest, a noted man of commerce, had a moment to think on the matter, the fiend danced past the spear and wheeled his monstrous axe in a great circle, the mask of Shrurosh leering in the moonlight, cleanly taking Earnest's head from his shoulders.

For a mere second, Earnest continued his forward trajectory, his body unaware that his skull had been severed from the torso. But then he slowed, stopped, and collapsed to the floor, much to the delight of the screaming crowd.

11

In the Wildings of Helmfirth

Lambert, of the family Philpot, took his seat and fixed his attention upon the vacant dais. He was an itinerant nibling of the same dynasty that innovated and distributed the dirigible, of which had quite famously propelled the Fair Isle of Gillion into the world with such ebullience. He was far from the bright lights of Arcton, many miles away from the filth and smog of the capital in the south. For a gentleman such as he, surrounded by many other puissant notables from across the country, to be partaking in such a scandalous affair, why it would have been the talk of the newspapers, both rag and respected, from Yarlford to Sartone, and everywhere in-between.

Lambert crossed his legs and adjusted the leather straps of his mask where it pinched. His was that of the Fox, the scavenger and most mischievous of the Hidden Spirits. The heat of that uncommonly sweltering autumn in the month of Gelan, even so far north, had cast the clearing in a damp mist. They were nestled within the wildings of Helmfirth, ten miles east of the mining village of Nantgarth, where his room waited in the only passable hotel for miles around. Lambert felt a trickle of sweat sliver down his spine. The temperature of his body ascended underneath his exquisite suit, procured from Proctor and Hobbs, a beautiful piece, but wholly unsuited to the odd climate.

They sat, those respectable, and in some cases notorious, few in a wide circle, bemasked and apprehensive, their many faces festooned with the beastly facades of the Hidden. The Fox that adorned Lambert, the Rabbit, the Badger, the Hedgehog, the Owl, and many more of the creatures of the forest. The gathered fidgeted in suits of fine materials and dresses of delicate fabrics as the tension escalated to its summit.

Lambert felt it in his stomach, and it surprised him. He usually had a cast-iron constitution and had anticipated being the last to feel the effects, but it appeared he was the first. It started deep within his bowels with a white-hot agony, causing him to grit his teeth. But the sensation was fleeting, to be replaced with a tingle that dispersed throughout his body until he felt as if his very epidermis rippled. Shortly, he noticed that the others around him had begun to react to the concoction in a comparable manner, with the lolling of heads and tapping of feet. But that was only the beginning.

As before, Lambert felt it first; the tingling, head lolling, and discomfort lifted, and the veil of the world lifted with it.

The towering trees that had kept watch around their seated persons, where before they were verdure shadows, abruptly became slender points of light. The night sky high above, where before was passing beyond dusk, now became a pinpricked wonder of stars, awash under an iridescent canopy.

Lambert felt both at peace and elated as the concoction took hold. He had been given a small glass filled with mushrooms of strange origins and fermented to a liquid. It tasted ghastly but it had done the trick. He glanced around at the faces of the others, and the masks bedizened with the Hidden came to life, moving and smiling, their wooden features exploding with expression.

As emotions continued to rise, the moment arrived.

Sitting upon the dais, Lambert saw a figure where before there was none.

Her hair, forged from the very fabric of nature and reminiscent of creeping vines, coquettishly cascaded down from her skull. Her orgone dress, fashioned from a kaleidoscope of flowers in an astonishing variety, fluttered as if propelled by a light breeze. Her sempiternal skin glistened, near pellucid, so clear Lambert could see her azure lifeblood as it pumped around her ethereal figure. Her dainty feet were bare.

"I," she proclaimed, her voice like the rustling of autumn leaves, "awaken."

Upon hearing her voice, Lambert and the others slipped from their chairs in adoration and came to their knees on the dirt of the forest floor. She glanced at their masked faces and smiled, causing the congregation to cry out in joy.

"Whom," she whispered, her voice now like the trickling of a babbling brook, "have you brought to me."

As soon as her words departed her sumptuous lips, the sacrifice was brought through the trees by men garbed in black, their faces obscured behind masks of dark velvet. They pushed through the gathered notables as they churned in ecstasy with a fair-haired boy in tow. They threw the winsome youth onto the wooden dais, where he writhed, unaware of his fate, his eyes unfocused, naked as the day he was born.

She peered down at the boy, her cherubic face serene, her hair swaying in the unearthly breeze, and smiled. Upon seeing her features contort as such, the distinguished gathered, including the jubilant Lambert, sobbed with glee.

"You," she remarked, her voice now like the pollinating winds on a fresh spring day, "have chosen wisely."

She then dropped to her knees and crawled towards the prone boy, her manner now primitive and base, her face now etched with esurience. The youth observed her approach with wide, terrified eyes, but he was wholly powerless to stop her.

She mounted him and placed her knees upon his shoulders, took his head lovingly in her hands, lowered her angelic face, and began to feast upon his flesh, while Lambert and the gathered watched in enraptured delight.

12

Beneath Proctor and Hobbs

As Riley wandered the cobbled streets of Arcton, passing through the mists and brume of an early morning, he mused about his life and how much it had changed. He had been apprenticing at Proctor and Hobbs for nearly six months, and it had been a rather illuminating experience. He thought back to the moment when his mother, the esteemed Lady Irvette Wiltone, arranged his position with the proprietors of that most respected establishment, and thanked his lucky stars. Mr Dalton Proctor and Mr Marshal Hobbs were two of the most revered businessmen in all of Gillion, and for him to be part of the company, and to be trained underneath those two masters, was quite the honour.

Riley turned another smog-laden street, weaving around a small but menacing crowd of labourers making their steady way to work, and wondered just how his mother had brokered the deal. He knew she was still in good standing with many of the most powerful families of Gillion, and that her, or should he say *their* name still held some water across the Fair Isle, and even in some states of Ecrium for that matter. But little did he know she still maintained enough sway to find him a position within the most celebrated of clothing companies.

He thought back on that fateful day. Lady Irvette had summoned Riley to the stately home in Calchester, which resided twenty miles west of the metropolis, and told him the news. Although it was only a half year prior, he already saw himself in a different light. He was a brash young man before, all vim and vigour, but with no direction. He had succoured his education at St. Haywood's Institute for Children, as his mother and grandfather did before him, but his grades, although passable, were far from exemplary. The situation had left him bereft of interest from the more cherished industries of Gillion. And largely bereft of his family's respect. In short, he had been rather flummoxed, but his mother, ever the assiduous type, had come to his rescue and called in some long-standing, but opaque, favours, allowing him to be taken under the wing of Mr Proctor and Mr Hobbs.

Riley had collected his meagre possessions from their estate and took the locomotive to the capital in somewhat of a daze. Yes, his dreams, although still somewhat nebulous to him at the time, were coming true, but when he had arrived, he found Arcton intimidating. The smog, the filth, the bustle of business, and the thronging crowds caused him to wonder on his, or should he say his mother's, decision to send him there, but she always knew what was best.

Riley strode along the cobbled roads, the vaporous sky above brightening at the fringes. His suit, an exquisite three-piece, provided for free by Mr Hobbs and Mr Proctor as part of his employment, a much-appreciated perk, was so finely made that the warmth of his body was clinging to his skin. In any normal circumstance, he would have slowed his march, but he found himself running short of time.

It wasn't entirely his fault. The 5:20 am omnibus had been late, but he highly doubted his employers would accept that as a viable excuse. If he was lucky, he would escape with a reprimand. If he was unlucky, he would be sweeping the manufactory floors, with the great behemoths of machinery that frequented the dark structure jangling his senses from dawn until the dusk. With only an old broom, used for such punishments as tardiness and oversights, for company.

With the thought of the penance and tongue-lashing that would accompany it, Riley practically jogged down Portmonth Road, sweat be damned, cursing his fate, his forehead creased with a frown. He splattered his brogues through the reeking puddles of the streets of Arcton, damaging the leather.

"Damn my miserable luck," angrily muttered Riley.

As he turned onto Dalefry Way, he saw the manufactory ahead, and, as always, it chilled his blood. There was something about the foreboding construction that caused his nerves to tingle. The dark stone, the jagged edges, and the dull metal, all amounted to a rather sinister frontage.

"I'm just being childish," he chided himself. "Why would it need to have a beautiful face like that of the National Gallery of Gillion or De Clare Theatre? It was a place of industry and business, not something for me to coo over like some naive neonate. My mother had always told me that I needed to detach my head from the clouds and away from poetry and silly notions, and onto the world of adulthood."

The building might have had a perfidious feel, but it contained the world-renowned Proctor and Hobbs, which produced the most delicate and inimitable garments, as well as the most fetching and decorous fashions for both the gentlemen and the gentlewomen of the Fair Isle. The seasonal lines of the company were the talk of not only the capital, but many of the countries of Ecrium, including far Sogristan, where they primarily dealt in furs.

But that wasn't the furthest regions those fine items found their way to. Riley had heard Mr Hobbs talking on the speaking telegraph about shipments being ordered from Esmia in the south continent, to chilly Etros in the distant northeast, and even to scattered, protectorate isles of the Westria beyond the Atlas Sea. There was even a whispered rumour of goods finding their way to Driuh Blana in Pestinia at the southernmost tip of Qathana, although he wouldn't have dared to add his voice to such scandalous talk. Either way, the company had an extraordinary reach.

The minutes were draining away, and Riley's reprimand was in danger of becoming severe. He continued to dash, grimacing in the heat, and passed through the open gates. He nodded at the uncouth, towering individual who operated the gate's clockwork controls and raced towards the office block to the left of the manufactory. That structure was slightly less threatening than its expansive sibling and was garnished with the name of the company in glittering golden font. He splashed through another pair of dark puddles and arrived at the office, bursting in through the oak wood doors, where he was met by a sea of raised eyes.

Riley's fellow administrators, fifteen in total, unfocused their gaze from the endless scribbling of ink on paper and watched his late arrival. One of them, the damnable Miss Alvena Turnbulle, glanced at the clock on the wall and smirked. She had never quite forgiven him for a drunken pass he made at her during a rather boozy work dinner in town. He had apologised for the slight, but she had never let it go. In his defence, at the time, being that it was the first week he lived in the city, he had been rather unused to strong spirits, and subsequently made a fool out of himself. The source of her current amusement was the time the clock read. It showed 7:10 am. He was ten minutes late. He prayed that Mr Hobbs wasn't there to witness his misstep.

But as Riley crept toward his desk in the colder portion of the office at the back of the room, as far away from the coal fire as possible due to his standing as the most recent apprentice of the company, he realised that wasn't the case.

"Mr Riley Wiltone, so good of you to join us. Why, pray tell, are you so late this morning?"

Riley stiffened, closing his eyes for a moment as if in pain. Mr Hobb's opprobrious voice cut through the air, followed by the intake of the breaths of many of his fellow administrators. Why did it have to be him, wondered Riley? Why couldn't it have been Mr Proctor? He was the more amiable of the two, and although firm, he could be fair. In contrast, the imperious Mr Hobbs had none of his finer qualities. Instead, he had a rather austere demeanour and could be outright bellicose when agitated.

When Riley saw Mr Hobb's gaunt features, he intuited that his employer wasn't in a forgiving mood. He was only a short fellow, and painfully slender, with only the merest smidgeon of hair upon his skull, but Riley found him daunting.

"Well, are you going to answer me?" barked Mr Hobbs.

It was all Riley could do to not tremble. "I... I'm sorry I'm late, sir," he squeaked. "The omnibus, sir, it was delayed on Snaton Cross..."

As Riley's weak fulmination died into silence, Mr Hobbs dark eyes remained locked upon him. "And do you believe that is enough of an excuse, Mr Wiltone? It seems to me that the others in this company have found the wit to make it here on time, and in some cases, at least an hour before." He glanced briefly at Riley's nemesis Alvena, who beamed at the meagre compliment. "So, why didn't you do the same? Why didn't you leave an hour earlier, thus avoiding such tardiness?"

Riley floundered on the spot with the eyes of Mr Hobbs lancing toward him. He opened his mouth to speak, but he was interrupted as soon as his lips parted.

"Lateness," spat Mr Hobbs, "is a disease, Mr Wiltone, one that must be treated with the correct remedy. Do you know what that is?"

Riley nodded his head, having been treated to the charade before.

"Go on, then," said Mr Hobbs, "tell the others."

"Lateness," recited Riley, his head bowed in shame, "can only be cured by hard work."

Mr Hobbs clicked his fingers, causing one of the nearest administrators to flinch. "That," he snapped, "is correct, Mr Wiltone. So, it appears that you can be taught something, after all. Well, since you're fully aware of the need for hard work, I believe you know what your job is going to be today?"

Riley's shoulders slumped in a saturnine manner. He knew there was no point arguing with Mr Hobbs. When he had made his decision, it was final, unless Mr Proctor came to his aid, which was a slim to nil hope at the best of times, but it appeared the fellow was away on business.

"Good, now get to it," commanded Mr Hobbs, turned on his heels, and went back into his office, slamming the door shut with a bang, which was followed by a rattling of pens and pencils in the holders on the desks nearest to his place of work.

Riley tramped through the office, chaperoned by mutters. He

took hold of the rickety broom that was set aside for such events and started towards the manufactory. He knew from experience the punishment was to completion. He was expected to catch up with the work he would miss later. It was going to be a long day.

By the time Riley completed the task the hours of light had slipped away. His mind was still fraught with the sound of the mechanical beasts that worked tirelessly all day and night, cutting the cloth that was procured from Westria that would become some of the finest fashions in the land. His hands were blistered from sweeping with the damnable broom. And to make matters worse, he had to remove a fair quantity of splinters from the bruised epidermis of his palms. And the final insult, his nose was filled with the stink of coal and petroleum as the gears and machinery ground their way through their artificial lives. It ran incessantly. In short, he was miserable.

Riley trudged back to the office, through the loading area, which was filled and emptied with horseless wagons all day, but by then it was quiet and largely vacant. It was past 9 pm and the place was deserted. Even the uncouth, towering gateman had vanished, leaving Riley locked inside, but that made no odds to him. He was going to be there overnight, whether he was trapped inside or not.

When he arrived in the office, Riley found it devoid of any administrators. His mood plummeted even further, but it did slightly rise when he saw that the gas lamps in Mr Hobbs office were also doused.

"Well, that's something, I guess," grumbled Riley, morose. "At least I can now work unencumbered."

He found his way to his desk at the back of the office, where it was still a good few degrees cooler than the rest of the room, and still falling with the onset of twilight, and wilted into his uncomfortable chair. The muscles of his legs thanked him for the respite, but his back still protested. He would dearly have loved to lie down for a time, but that would have been impossible. If he was to rest for even a moment, he might never wake until the morning. He shuddered to think what would have happened if he hadn't completed his daily work. Or even worse, what Mr Hobbs would have done if he found him asleep in the office. It didn't bear thinking about.

No, Riley had work to do, so he brewed himself a cup of tea using the pot provided by the company, another perk, and set to it.

The hours seemed to vanish, and the night became deep. Riley heard nothing of the outside world within his cocoon. No one came to check on him, which seemed like a rather strange oversight. Surely the night watchman or another some such fellow should have been patrolling the manufactory? Riley was certain during his last infraction and subsequent punishment that was the case. Whoever the person was, they were in even greater danger than he. Leaving the manufactory unattended was surely a dismissible offence. And if you were fired from Proctor and Hobbs, you were sure to never work in Arcton again. Your best course of action would have been to retreat to the cold north of Gillion, where the pay was less, and the weather was worse. If it ever happened to him, his mother would have simply never forgiven him. And worse, he would have been in danger of being cut off. He shuddered at the thought.

Despite his numb fingers and his aching back, Riley, his face ashen, had worked studiously through his tasks. Apparently, a near-debilitating cold keeps a fellow rather fresh and awake. He turned his final page and added it to the pile to his left with a little flourish. That was the end of what would normally be his daily tasks, and he had to say, without the distractions of the office, and the dread that Mr Hobbs might make an appearance, he found he worked quite diligently on his own. It was just a shame no one was there to witness his small victory. If only there was a way to prove he had not only completed his penalty, but his other work, and in good time, so he could demonstrate to both Mr Hobbs and Mr Proctor that he wasn't entirely useless.

A clever notion came to Riley, then. He knew the perfect way he could prove he was a worthwhile employee and someone who would go the extra mile when needed. Someone who could be relied upon in any situation. The nightwatchman had almost certainly not shown in for the night, leaving the manufactory open to burglary. This was his chance, he concluded. If he spent the rest of the night, which was only a few more hours anyway, patrolling the manufactory and making sure there were no uninvited guests, and then reported back to Mr Hobbs in the morning, he would surely be allowed some reprieve from the man's wrath.

"Yes, it's a wonderful idea," said Riley with gusto.

His mother had told him he needed to be resourceful in the company. The implementation of his plan might show her he could be just that. With the certitude that his scheme was sound, he clambered onto his exhausted feet, spending a little time stretching his back and rubbing warmth back into his numb legs, and then set to the task, throwing on his suit jacket for protection against the nightly chill.

Riley grabbed a gaslamp, lit the wick, departed the relative warmth of the office, and plunged into the night. His breath fogging, he patrolled the outer borders of the manufactory. The cold nipped, but he kept moving and made swift work of the task to discover there was still no one about, not even at the gates. He ventured inside, which appeared to be no warmer than the outside. Here, he slowed to a bewildered halt. There was something different inside. It took him a few moments to realise what it was. It was the titanic machines. They were all silent, inert, and undoubtedly idle.

Riley was confident he had been told on many occasions that those great brutish beasts of metal and innovation worked throughout the night, but that didn't appear to be the case. How or why, he had no idea, but it wasn't his place to question the authority of his employer. No, he just needed to be a reliable sort. With that in mind, he began to comb the manufactory, wandering in and out of the indolent iron and steel machinery. Due to the hush, his footsteps sang out in the open space as he wandered those strange corridors of industry.

The manufactory was enormous, and a full pass would take quite some time, but about halfway through his patrol Riley heard the most irregular sound. It came to his ears at the southernmost point of the building. His first thoughts went to the dramatic.

"Is that an intruder?" whispered Riley, confidence in his plan evaporating.

He crept towards the noise, which sounded like nothing more than the tolling of distant hammers. As he approached, the sound was joined by a tremoring underfoot and the soft glow of gaslamp light. He came to a door, slightly ajar, from which the sound and light were emanating. That close, he heard the clang of metal on metal, a dull, repetitive thudding.

At first, Riley baulked at the prospect, but he recalled why he was there. If it was, in fact, thieves, and he caught them red-handed, he would be a hero to Mr Hobbs and Mr Proctor, and all his past infractions, however large or small, would be forgiven. With that firmly in mind, he nudged open the door and peered inside. There, he found a staircase. With each downward step, the ringing of metal grew in volume and seemed to reverberate off the stone walls.

All was cast in darkness. The staircase was devoid of gaslamps or any other source of light, but the faint lambent that Riley had detected on the manufactory floor grew as he rambled ever downwards, amalgamating its light with his own gaslamp. As he descended, the knell of metal became louder still, and a dry heat rose. Where before, he was nearly numb with the chill, he now found his forehead was pricked with perspiration. Was there a forge down there of some kind? Or some other source of heat? If so, he had never heard of such a thing.

With curiosity driving him, Riley slipped down the steps. When he arrived at the bottom of the staircase, he emerged out into a space so astonishing that he nearly dropped his gaslamp onto the floor and involuntary hissed his breath inwards.

"Well, I never," he said in awe.

Riley had come out at the top of a vast, open space. He stood in an expansive room made of the same dark stone as the manufactory above. In some ways, it was also a manufactory, but one he had never heard about nor seen mentioned anywhere in Arcton.

Stranger still, sitting in the centre of the expansive space, and the source of both the light, heat, and noise, was something Riley could only describe as a vast spider wrought from machinery so enormous, so gigantic, his mind simply couldn't process what it saw. The spider, and he used the term loosely since it only resembled an arachnid in the sense that it had many legs which protruded from a focal, solid bulk, tirelessly worked away. It laboured in tandem with many other small machines that surrounded it like its diminutive minions, connected to it via many lengths of wire. The machine cut and stripped cloth and then weaved and stitched them together at a staggering rate.

The metal giant performed the task that its simple counterparts were doing upstairs, but far, far more efficiently. It churned out the cloth needed for the company at an incredible speed, lifting them from great containers at the periphery of the manufactory floor and then either inserted it within its bulk or sent them to different parts of the rooms to its many automatronic minions to do with them what they would.

In short, the machine was a wonder, one that Riley had never thought he would ever see, but due to its mechanical movements, he found that he trembled to be near the thing. It then occurred to him that no one had ever spoken about the great machine before and that it might be a secret. As for why, he had no idea, as surely Mr Hobbs and Mr Proctor would want everyone in Gillion to know of such a wonderous appliance. Why, he realised, it would revolutionise the industry. Although the fuel alone to power such a machine would cost a pretty penny and it would be an industry in of itself just to maintain the thing.

For a time, Riley stood and wondered how it all worked, but then he came to his senses. It was not for such as him to pry. He shouldn't be there, and he thought it would be best to leave. He took one last look at the titanic spider and turned to leave, but ground to a halt when a familiar voice startled him.

"Now, what might you be doing down here, Mr Wiltone?"

Mr Hobbs' voice punctured the endless noise of the spider and caused Riley's blood to run cold. He met his employer's eyes as they narrowed. He began to utter his defence, but a sharp pain sprang at the back of his skull, followed by darkness.

When Riley came to, he found he was on the warm floor. He prised his moist cheek from the stone, flinching with pain from the blow. He rolled onto his back and fingered the dried blood on the back of his skull, but winced away again when he saw the enormous metal brute above move, going about its business. So close to the miscreation, the sound was abrasive to his ears, but that wasn't the only noise he heard. There was something else, something more rhythmic nearby that didn't make sense to him.

A familiar voice spoke over the din.

"So, you found our little secret then, did you, Mr Wiltone? Your mother will be deeply unhappy when we tell her, but she will understand, I'm sure. She has a great deal of money invested in the company, and she would not be pleased if this got out. Which puts us in a bit of a pickle."

Riley followed the sound of Mr Proctor's voice and found him standing next to Mr Hobbs with his hands clasped behind his back, their foreheads glistening with sweat. Mr Proctor was the antithesis of his partner in business. Whereas Mr Hobbs was gaunt and pallid, Mr Proctor was rotund and ruddy-cheeked. Whereas Mr Hobbs' hair was thinning away to nothing, Mr Proctor's was thick and voluminous. They both wore tailored suits of the finest quality, but that was the only likeness they shared. Mr Hobbs glowered in his usual fashion, but Mr Proctor appeared somewhat lugubrious.

Mr Proctor turned to his colleague. "What shall we do we him, Mr Hobbs?" he bellowed over the racket of machinery.

"I think you know, Mr Proctor," shouted Mr Hobbs in reply.

Mr Proctor shook his head sadly. "He's right, but this is the way it has to be, I'm afraid." He nodded. "Mr Reevese, if you would."

The uncouth, hulking gateman appeared and strode toward Riley. He tried to scramble away, but the brute was swift, and before he had a moment to think, he was hauled across the floor, protesting with each step, towards the spider. Mr Hobbs and Mr Proctor joined him, flanking them both.

"I am sorry about this, Mr Wiltone," called Mr Proctor. "I will have to personally apologise to Iverette. She will be displeased, but as I've already said, she'll understand, and she's quite a sweety. You caught us at a rather inopportune time, you see. We were just conducting some maintenance with the help of Mr Reevese. It was an awful bother, but I'm afraid to say it caused Mr Hobbs to forget that you were still here. It's a terrible business, really, but what's done is done. As for you, you will continue to serve the company, but in more, shall we say, trying working conditions."

At that, Mr Hobbs chuckled.

Riley tried to grapple with what they were telling him. All the while, he was heaved to the spider, his face drawn with terror. Up close, the machine was horribly hot, and the air was a stifling taint that sat heavily on his chest. He peered around, his eyes agog, trying to get a sense of his predicament, but that was when he spied the others.

Beside the bulk of the metal spider was the most peculiar device. Upon seeing it, Riley was reminded of the older modes of transport, the humble galleon, long before the dirigible and locomotive, when slaves were procured from Qathana. He remembered seeing pictures of those rowing boats that were powered by the brute force of many men. One such device had been inserted into the bulk of the vast machine, and working it were a great many men and women. They wore nothing but filthy, tattered rags, their bodies glittering with muck and sweat, painfully thin. They powered the machine with their collective strength, rowing in rhythm, flanked by an individual clad in black, his hood pulled up and obscuring his features. He brandished a whip while wandering the lines, viciously putting forth his authority.

Riley's cerebrum strained under the terror, his mind unable to grasp his doom, but then it suddenly hit him.

Their fate was now his own.

Riley struggled, but Mr Reevese held him fast. When he was dragged, kicking and screaming, to the contraption, the brute was joined by the swine dressed in black, and they teamed to throw him into a vacant spot, locking the manacles around both his legs and wrists. With their job done, they stepped back and regarded their handiwork while Mr Hobbs and Mr Proctor watched on.

In his fear, Riley finally found some coherent words. "You can't do this," he weakly protested.

"Nonsense. Of course, we can," replied Mr Hobbs. "Now, you best get to work."

He nodded to the beast with the whip, who flicked it in Riley's direction. It was only a glancing blow, but it served to send agony across his cheek, and he squealed in pain. He dallied only a moment when the beast brandished the whip again and then joined in the rhythmic rowing of the others.

"Good," said Mr Proctor with a wry grin, "you've picked it up already. Your mother will be delighted to see that you're finally applying yourself. Anyway, we must be off."

For a moment, Mr Proctor and Mr Hobbs stood side by side, each the antithesis of the other, and peered at Riley. He gawped at them, hoping beyond hope that it was all some clever jest, a rouse of some kind, but they didn't utter another word. Then, to Riley's amazement, both Mr Proctor and Mr Hobbs' eyes briefly glittered ruby red. He was dumbfounded. The pair then turned and departed together with Mr Reevese, leaving the monster with the whip looming over him.

Riley was trapped, and there was nothing he could do. Sweat already leaked from every pore. He joined his strength with the other poor souls and powered the hulking spider of machinery as it endlessly churned out clothing for the most famous company in all the land, Proctor and Hobbs.

13

The Long Smog

Day 1,
Rhosday 12th Corasil

Dr Thorley has asked me to keep a diary and track my progress for the next two weeks, so consider this the beginning of the diary of myself, Victor Bowditch, in the year 4799.

The day had started out poorly. The journey in the omnibus had been as tiresome as to be expected. I knew it was going to be a mistake. I don't know why I didn't just hire a horseless carriage, but I like to frequent the public transport every now and then and give a little back to the nation, and this was one of those days. Predictably, it was packed with commuters making their way to work on a dreary Rhosday morning and consequently, it was stifling.

I just had to make do with sweating profusely in the near unbearable heat, hoping that I didn't ruin my suit, and trying to adjust my respi-

ration mask in vain, of which I didn't dare take off. I'm thoroughly aware that these masks are essential, and I've read all the literature on the subject, but that doesn't stop me from constantly wishing that I could just simply rip the blasted contraption off and cast it away. But of course, that would be ridiculous. I'd be on the floor in seconds, choking on the miasma-saturated air of Arcton, and probably blubbering and sobbing in terror until someone saved me. I'd rather avoid that embarrassment if at all possible. Still, the bloody thing does pinch so.

After a brief but arduous trip, I had arrived at the Gillion Research Centre for Botany. I have to say, it was quite a sight to behold. It's a remarkable building. It reminded me of some of the architecture of the ancient world, around the Meshil Sea, perhaps fashioned after the structures of ancient Naptriule and Asnary, with its impressive columns and tall façade. It really was a glorious sight.

And then, the first shock.

I was told I would be met by the veritable Doctor who would then escort me inside. This was a precautionary measure, as the procedure is still in its infancy and strictly by invitation only, this being one of the first rounds of testing. I could and can still see sense in that. If word were to get out, there would be uproar, and an eager mob would form within seconds. The snollygosters in Parliament need to tread exceedingly carefully with this matter. Of course, I was sworn to secrecy, which, being that I'm a loyal citizen, wasn't really necessary because I do know my place.

Anyway, I digress. Dr Thorley came to meet me at the front of the building with his head exposed and a cheerful grin on his lean face.

I yelped in terror and nearly rushed at the man, thinking that he'd misplaced his mask and that I would be needed to help him safely back inside, but then I remembered why I was there and held my tongue.

He strode right to me and took my trembling hand in his. "Good morning, Mr Bowditch, is it? Victor Bowditch? It's a pleasure to make your acquaintance," he said to me, and I have to admit I was at a loss for words.

Any reservations about the procedure evaporated in that moment. There was the good Dr Thorley, a man of science, outside in the fume-soaked atmosphere, no mask in sight, and seemingly in perfect health. My enthusiasm reached its zenith.

I was ushered inside, where I removed my own mask and was dizzily led through squeaky clean corridors, while the virtuous Dr Thorley dutifully filled me in. I could barely follow what he was saying. My mind was firmly on the fact of his being able to breathe unfiltered, and I simply couldn't focus on his words. It has been many a month since I've been able to be outside without a mask on. It already seems a bit like a dream of a dream when we could breathe the fresh air unaided in the capital, before the smog came, and not feel any ill effects, or at least only a few minor consequences. It seemed to come on so gradually that I don't believe people truly understood that all our industry here in Arcton was clogging up the skies with dangerous vapours until it was too late. Of course, there are calls to slow the business of the nation, but it's been stuck in Parliament for weeks now, and there seems to be no end in sight. And this may be the only currently viable alternative.

Eventually, we reached Doctor Thorley's laboratory, where I was asked to sit with a small group of others, maybe twenty in total. They appeared as flabbergasted as myself, judging by their wide, gawping eyes.

There, we were treated to a whistle-stop presentation of what I must say is the discovery of the decade. I'll briefly surmise, although it's unnecessary for this diary, but I'd like to get it down on paper for posterity. Around an ancient meteor site in the sweltering southern hemisphere, in the continent of Qathana, in a country whose name I couldn't possibly pronounce, and deep in the bowels of an occasionally active volcano, the noble Dr Thorley and his band of researchers had found a hardy, miniature plant that can grow in any conditions. As if this wasn't uncommon enough, and what makes this plant, or Mundus Alius Spirara as it's known scientifically, so extraordinary, is just how much it flourishes. This tiny botanical grows in riotous abundance, soaking in the noxious air of the volcano greedily.

In his infinite wisdom, Dr Thorley deracinated samples of this astonishing breakthrough and returned to the Fair Isle forthwith to test his discovery. What he found was that the organism will grow anywhere and in any environment, with or without the usual necessities for vegetation. Namely, water and sunlight. And crucially, it absorbs the smog and excretes oxygen efficiently, if not more so than any other plant that can be found on Yuthea.

Fast forward a year and some clever science from the esteemed Dr Thorley, along with some heavy funding from Her Majesty's Parliament, and there we have it: Spiraramine. A tiny seed in the form of a pill that can be implanted, excuse the pun, where this wonderful, lifesaving flower can grow in your lungs, so that we can walk around outside in Arcton without the need for the irksome respirator masks. I'm told the roots attach themselves to the walls of the lungs, bloom, and then get to work. I'm also reliably informed that it's perfectly safe and judging by the show that Dr Thorley put on when I first arrived, I'm inclined to believe him.

Needless to say, everyone in the room, including myself, readily agreed to be the first test subjects for the good of Arcton.

Day 3,
Ebrisday 14th Corasil

Dr Thorley informed me I'd feel the effects within a few days, but I have to admit that after I'd come down from the thrill and excitement of the introductory presentation, I started to doubt the truth of it. If I'm being honest, I've always been a distrusting sort of fellow, which might explain why I never married or had children, despite having the capital to do so. I was lucky that my parents left me quite the inheritance when they passed on from a rather vile ague epidemic that beleaguered Gillion for many months a decade ago, but I've never really done anything with it.

Now that I come to think about it, I may have wasted my youth on mere pleasure, taking trips to Ecrium and even further afield to Etros and Westria, indulging in revelry and suchlike, but I don't particularly regret my decisions. Living in this chaotic world is insuperable enough without having others to worry about. I do own a house cat, but I don't often see the old feline. Osbert spends his days rattling around the house in one of the many bedrooms hunting for mice and insects. He appears to be doing a decent job, as I've not seen any pests for months, although that might be more to do with the pernicious atmosphere than the cat's prowess.

But I digress. I need to remember this diary is for the reporting of any side effects and the progress of the Spiraramine, and not whatever comes into my wandering mind.

So, down to business.

Firstly, it's a miracle.

Really, truly.

After the first day, I felt different. Energised somehow. I don't know if that was just simple ebullience or not, but I felt and feel invigorated. After the short, but excruciating, procedure at the Research Centre where the pill was inserted, or perhaps I should say, rammed down my throat by a lengthy and sinister-looking contraption made from glittering steel, I returned home with some esoteric literature. It states that I should wait a few days and then, if possible, head outside in secret and test it out, but to always keep my respiration mask handy, just in case.

I did as instructed, but on the second morning, I couldn't contain myself any longer. I'm lucky that due to the amble grounds that encase my home, secrecy isn't an issue. So, I ventured outside with my mask firmly fixed to my sweating face and my heart thumping in my chest. I wandered down the gravel path and found a bench near the ornate sundial which frequents that portion of the grounds, only fifty metres from the back door, and sat down. My hand trembled when I removed my mask, and I instinctively held my breath, but after a short time, I couldn't bear it any longer, and I took one quick frantic breath.

To my utter astonishment, I didn't choke and splutter. No, instead, I took a deep lung full, inhaling and exhaling, as if it was the most perfectly normal thing in the world. The process was instantaneous and evidently seamless.

Spiraramine works!

I remained there for the rest of the day, just sitting and breathing and doing nothing more. My respiration mask, with its leather casing, glass frontage, and metal and plastic straps, a forgotten and obsolete relic by my side.

Of course, I venture out of the city from time to time, especially beyond the capital's boundaries and occasionally to the north of Gillion, where there's little or no smog, but being in my family home, in the grounds, and without a mask was a revelation.

I sat for many hours outside today and watched the blazing sun rise steadily into the air and allowed it to warm my face, it even burnt it a little, but I didn't care. I watched as it rose, and then set, plunging the polluted, cloud-laden sky into a titian and crimson landscape. At one point, the world wore a scarlet mask that made the grounds that encircle my home, with its stone surfaces, lush foliage, and verdant swards, look magnificent.

That night I slept so soundly that I barely dreamt, and I awoke this morning more galvanised than ever. The city is suddenly open to me now in a way that I haven't experienced in months. The urge to rush out and head to town is powerful, but I know my duty. For the good of Gillion, I'll do as I was told and furtively remain here.

Day 5,
Ixday 16th Corasil

I had the most peculiar dream last night. In it, I traversed a thoroughly alien landscape. The world of my unconscious was sumptuous and filled with such dense flora that my rational mind could barely comprehend what I was seeing. As I walked, I became aware that I wasn't wearing my respiration mask, but then, in that strange way of slumber, I promptly realised I didn't need it. Not only that, but I would never need it again. I felt great delight at that fact.

I continued to wander that overgrown world, and it suddenly struck me just how vivid my dream was. Usually, I can't remember what's happened even a moment before, or I quickly move on to another segment of my inner mind, but that never materialised. Instead, I just wandered through that verdant world agape at the wildlife and vegetation that was in such plenty that my mind boggled.

That on its own was strange enough, but towards the end of what felt like a lifetime of exploring that viridescent land, I had the oddest feeling like I'd been there before. It was very similar to déjà vu, but

I'm sure I've never had that sensation in a dream before. There was something familiar and yet unfamiliar about it all. I'm not sure if this counts as a side effect or not, but I'll leave it in here regardless.

Anyway, back to the job at hand.

I've spent the last two days roving and rambling in the grounds without my mask, and in those days, I've found peace. I hadn't realised just how anxious I've become in my middling years until now. Yes, my temples are beginning to grey, and my forehead is forming a permanent etching in the skin, but I always just assumed that a torpid demeanour was part of a person's dotage. But I was wrong. I feel younger somehow, more virile even.

The anxiety of living in this bustling city has been weighing me down for years without even realising it. And then the smog came and made it far, far worse. Now that that tension has lifted, I find that I want to live. I even want to love. Although this is highly personal, and certainly not something that I would typically divulge in polite company, I masturbated for the first time in I don't know how long yesterday. The urge just suddenly came over me. I only mention it because it may also be a side effect of the Spiraramine, but it equally might just be the feeling of liberation.

I even ventured out for a time into Arcton, but I quickly returned because I couldn't stand wearing my mask any longer. I felt so restrictive and uncomfortable, even more than it ever did before. I have to say that I practically sprinted back to the house from the horseless carriage. I must have looked a fool, but I didn't care. I <u>needed</u> to be back and remove my mask forthwith. I hope the day swiftly comes when I can permanently throw the vile thing in the *bin, and not just me, but everyone else in the capital.*

And what a day that will be.

Day 7,
Irasday 18th Corasil

The strangest thing happened today.

I had put it off longer than I usually do, but I ordered a horseless carriage, rather than taking the odious omnibus, and went into the city. The district of Harcaster Heath isn't an overly beautiful area, although it certainly has its moments, but I had the most powerful of urges to be around other people. The impulse was so ardent I didn't even mind wearing my mask despite not needing the wretched thing.

I meandered the cobbled streets for a few hours without any real destination in mind, when I happened upon one of my favourite haunts, a public house by the name of The Jolly Isle. My feet seemed to have led me there without my mind's knowledge, but it was a happy coincidence as I was famished after a day on my feet.

I took a seat near the window, ordered a pint and a plate of cheese and crackers, and spent the next hour leisurely reading the local paper, the Harcaster Journal, a thoroughly mediocre broadsheet, but the only passable one the district has to offer, when it happened.

A young lady approached my table entirely uninvited and took the seat next to mine. She was a slender slip of a woman, but winsome in an everyday sort of way, although her complexion was quite drawn. As you can imagine, I was quite taken aback at first, but then the most unusual realisation spread through me. I instinctively knew that she'd taken Spiraramine. I don't think I could adequately explain why, but it was just a pure certitude that settled into my mind.

She regarded me for a moment and then shyly whispered in my ear.

"You've had it, haven't you?" she said.

I folded my newspaper and carefully laid it down on the table, more to buy myself some time as I don't ordinally speak to strangers in such a manner, but for some unknown reason, I felt perfectly at ease.

I smiled and told her that I had indeed taken it, whereupon she grabbed my hand and squeezed it tightly.

"It's wonderful, isn't it? Truly wonderful," she giddily said.

Of course, I agreed.

"When did you get it?" she enthusiastically continued. "Three weeks ago, or four? I was in the first test group three weeks ago. It's changed my life."

Now, that was confusing. I quietly informed her that I had taken it only a week before, but she didn't seem too perturbed by this information. I had no idea that there are other test groups taking

Spiraramine, and I have to say I was a little surprised, but that soon turned to curiosity. I asked her how she felt.

She smiled beatifically and squeezed my hand tighter. "Wonderful. I've never felt like this before in my life."

Now, what I'm about to disclose is an exceedingly personal matter, but I shall forge on regardless. At that moment, I was overcome by an intense arousal. With barely another word said, I paid the bill and ordered another horseless carriage. We departed and returned to my home, where we proceeded to indulge in a debauched night of sexual congress, the likes of which I've never been party to before. When we had finished, she informed me that she, too, had never indulged in a night like we just had and was as puzzled about the whole sleazy affair as I was.

Something had been playing on my mind, so I asked her how she knew that I had taken Spiraramine, to which she shrugged.

"I just did, but I honestly don't know why," she said, and left shortly afterwards, leaving me to wonder whether I'd taken leave of my senses.

I only recount this sordid tale to you not out of vaingloriousness but due to the inexplicable connection that we seemingly found within moments of meeting each other. I've no idea if it's important or not, but I felt like it was worth divulging.

Day 9,
Fetherday 20th Corasil

I write in this diary at an ungodly hour.

It's the middle of the night. 3:42 am, to be exact. I've been thrust into the wakeful world by the most irregular of dreams, even more so than the recent ones where I strolled through a lush alien world that I've visited on more than one occasion in the last few days. In it, I floated in a wide lake cast in verdigris, surrounded by an astoundingly dense forest under an unfamiliar and uncracked moon. It was a tranquil place, and I felt immediately at peace, but after a short time, I gradually came to be aware that I wasn't the only person there.

Appearing as if by some unknown force, I came to the realisation that the lake was filled with many hundreds of others who each were floating in the water the same as myself. I watched as we all mutely noted each other's presence, but there was no definition to our bodies. No lips to speak or eyes to see. We were simply beings of effervescent energy bobbing in the azure water.

For a time, I wondered why we were there, but then, a soothing voice seemed to descend and filled our minds. I can't remember their exact words, but they spoke of the majesty of the universe and the beauty in its vastness, but they explained that the size was also a curse. It enquired whether we understood that the cosmos would be a better place if the many worlds that were spread throughout its trilliard of galaxies were all connected somehow. I, as well as the others, agreed that it would indeed be a much-improved situation, and the voice seemed happy with that response. The last words it spoke I do remember clearly. They have plagued my mind ever since.

"It will soon be time," it said.

I don't know what this all means, but the certainty of the truth of that comment, however odd, filled my whole being and is with me still.

I mention this again because I'm beginning to worry that there's more to these strange dreams and that they're in some way connected to Spiraramine. Perhaps I'm mistaken, but I've never experienced anything like them before.

Soon I will return to the Research Centre, and it can't come soon enough. As much as I enjoy my time outside, I fear the night and what it brings. I can't adequately explain myself, but a feeling of dread has settled into my soul over the last few days that no amount of time outside in the open air can satisfactorily shake. Moreover, my primal, sensual urges are so extreme that I masturbate constantly and continually think back to my tryst with the stranger from The Jolly Isle, but I never seem to be satisfied.

Also, if I don't make an effort to keep my emotions in check, I hastily grow angry at the most banal of things. The other day, I smashed a cup for no more reason than the tea it contained had gone cold while I'd daydreamed with it in my hand.

I wonder, is this normal?

Day 11,
Athosday 22nd Corasil

I didn't sleep a wink last night.

When I ventured to bed at the usual time, I just laid awake for hours, my mind ablaze with a milliard of uncanny thoughts and strange notions, but sleep was an old friend whose speaking telegraph number I'd forgotten, condemning me to never converse with them again.

At first, I didn't mind this fact as I fear the unsettling dreams, but the oddest part about it was that after I'd been up for the entire night, I felt no ill effects. I sit here now, nearly forty-eight hours since I've last slept, and I feel entirely comfortable. I've spent most of that time outside in the air, breathing deeply. What's more, I feel like....

No, I know something is about to happen, but as for what, I've simply no idea.

As if all that wasn't extraordinary enough, I've barely eaten in the last four or five days. Food just doesn't seem to sit well with me. I note it here because I believe this to be a side effect as I've always had a healthy appetite, which has negatively affected my waistline over the years. Since I've not been eating as much, my weight has dropped, so I guess that could be considered a positive benefit?

Soon, and I will be able to return to the Research Centre and relay this odd behaviour. For the moment, I will have to spend another day with myself and the unusual thoughts that seem to inhabit my mind as of late.

Day 13,
Withday 24th Corasil

Light has not yet broken.

I haven't slept for days, but I feel stronger somehow, fitter, and healthier than ever before in my life. My body feels supple and robust and filled with life, despite the lack of nourishment. I have to say the slim individual I see in the mirror every morning reminds me of myself when I was a youthful lad, filled with vim and vigour, and not the doughy middle-aged man I'd become.

I had a waking dream last night. One moment I was walking along a corridor in my home with a mind to make a cup of tea, and the next, I was transported to a familiar place. Again, I had returned to the indigo lake, but it wasn't the dead of night. This time, I swam underneath two suns ablaze in a sapphire sky, one vaster, brilliantly white, and starkly prominent, while the other, a lesser star cast in a deep crimson.

As I bobbed in the water, I could feel the others all around me, and I knew that we'd swollen in numbers. Where before there were hundreds, now there were thousands, maybe more. I came to realise that we were all waiting for the voice to return, and when it did, I felt such joy I thought I might extemporaneously combust.

This time, I remember their words, so I've copied it here, verbatim.

"The time is coming very soon, my children. Tomorrow, we rise. Tomorrow, we begin. Tomorrow, the future dawns. Do you understand?" it said.

We mutely agreed that we did, and I do believe that I do understand now.

The voice continued. Tomorrow, my children. Tomorrow.

At that moment, the lake and wilding world faded, and I was swiftly returned to the corridor in my house.

I've spent the last few hours thinking on this, and what these mysterious thoughts that have invaded my mind as of late. I seem to know things that I shouldn't.

Here is a selection of them:

I know of Audrey Gladwine, who works as an accountant in the city. She received Spiraramine a month ago and has since been outside on many occasions without her mask and frequently taken lovers. At first, she feared what was happening to her, but now she has accepted it as the gift that it is.

I know of Wystan Browne, who works at pharmaceuticals in the east Arcton district of Merton. He took his pill a week ago and was terrified at first, but quickly warmed to his new predicament. He's upset that his wife still shows no interest in taking it, but has resigned himself to doing something about it, although not until the time is right.

I also know of Wilfred Hilton, a grocer, who lives in the port town of Sudbury. He took his Spiraramine twelve weeks ago and has not slept for eight of those weeks but finds that he doesn't need it anymore. He has taken many lovers and eagerly awaits tomorrow.

Norma Heathe, an omnibus driver who lives in the Lybster district. She despises her passengers but doesn't let that cloud her happiness that they'll soon be liberated.

Stuart Westbrooke, an administrator at a branch of Gillion Bank in Rachdale, a town a mere few miles from the capital. He eagerly awaits liberation, but he's also nervous about his two children.

Beverly Winfielde from district of Ely was anxious about her children as well, but she convinced her husband to take them all to the Research Centre two weeks ago, and now they're all happy together.

And I know of Dr Thorley, the first person to take the wonder drug six months ago. I know that he's spent that time giving it to many hundreds of patients, as well as other doctors and a few Parliamentarians across the city, who in turn have then begun distributing it themselves, so they now know the joy that it brings. I know that he's known for many months what Spiraramine can do and frequently convenes with the others.

And finally, I know of the Supreme Mother. She has watched over the universe for a milliard of years and has been enacting her plan for almost as much time. I know that in her infinite wisdom, she has sent a trilliard of projectiles out into the void, each protecting a spore that when it meets the correct conditions, it can grow and flourish and become a splendid flower. I know that when ingested, the beautiful blossom can merge with its host, and that it can be passed on via sexual congress. I know that this wonder of a remedy can also reveal Her plan, and with it comes liberation.

I also know that there will be some who will fight against the emancipation to come. If only they knew, then they would understand, but they're unable to comprehend true freedom as I do now.

But it's too late for them.

Day 14,
Irasday 25th Corasil

It is today.

Today, we begin the liberation of Gillion.

The Supreme Mother has wished it so, and now it will come to pass.

I must join the rest of my family, my brothers and sisters, as we reveal ourselves to the world.

It will begin with Arcton, but from here, we will take over the country, and then join the others and take the world.

About the Author

Elliot Harper is a speculative fiction writer who lives in Leeds, England.

He is the author of the science-fiction and fantasy novel, New Gillion Street, published by Fly on the Wall Press.

His short story, *In the Garden*, won the Flash Vision 2021 flash fiction contest by The Molotov Cocktail magazine.

His short story, *Meme*, was nominated for the Pushcart Prize in 2021 by Coffin Bell Journal.

He has short stories in print as follows: *The Curious Case of the Speaking Telegraph* in the *Spirit Machine: Tales of Seance Fiction* anthology by Air and Nothingness Press, *Into the Forest* in *The Wild Hunt: Stories of the Chase* anthology by Air and Nothingness Press, *There's a Dead Bear in the Pool* in *Black Telephone* Issue 1 by

Clash Books, *Blackout* in The *Protest Issue* of Popshot Quarterly Magazine.

He has various 26 short stories online in Maudlin House, Storgy, Akashic Books Sci-fi Friday, Neon Books, Ghost City Press, Coffin Bell, Five:2:One, Dream Noir, Litro Magazine, Horrified Magazine and Idle Ink.

You can connect with me on:

https://www.elliotjharper.com

Also by Elliot J Harper

New Gillion Street

In politically-neutral Neo-Yuthea, Albert Smith's orderly life is disrupted when Mr. Zand campaigns for Mayor, leading to uncertain times. Shocking deaths caused by strange forest creatures, enforced arranged marriages, and the impending suppression of Albert's secret garden meetings bring the community to the brink of chaos. Albert and his neighbours must rally together, resisting the encroaching darkness and fighting for their freedom before their world crumbles.

Printed in Great Britain
by Amazon

53010196R00086